SUMMER OF THE LONG KNIVES

Praise for *Summer of the Long Knives*:

Summer of the Long Knives packs so much into a short space. The background of 1930s Berlin creates depth, the characters' colour, the plot style, and excitement. L.B. handles all of her elements very nicely indeed.

–Iain Pears, English art historian, journalist,
author of *An Instance of the Fingerpost,*
The Dream of Scipio, The Portrait,
and *Stone's Fall*

I was so caught up in *Summer of the Long Knives* that I read it like a thriller, while being imaginatively influenced by it like a dream. I was delighted by the sureness of tone and familiarity with the facts, by the subtlety of the characterization – and especially by Lisel's character development – and by the pattern of poetic images that accumulated just in the tail of one's eye, so to speak. Also, the marvelous historical imagination. It was more serious, in the best sense, than almost every other contemporary novel I've read. I've almost given up reading contemporary novels for that reason – they have no moral depth, no interest beside the confirmation of whatever nasty little compromises one had made in one's own life. But *Summer of the Long Knives*, without any preaching, and in the lightest, more ironical way, really hits the great and terrible issues of our time. The novel is also an extraordinary experiment in what George Steiner has called *alternity*: for Bassen, time has a complex geometry in which alternative branches of it can morally influence each other. So the novel also has a philosophical depth that makes it unusual.

– Frederick Turner, Founders Professor of Arts and Humanities at the University of Texas at Dallas

Summer of the Long Knives is an utterly gripping and original novel of alternate history. I could not put it down.

– Stephanie Cowell, author of *Claude & Camille: A Novel of Monet.*

SUMMER OF THE LONG KNIVES

A novel

L.S. BASSEN

Signal 8 Press (Lightning Originals)
Hong Kong

Summer of the Long Knives
By LS Bassen
Published by Signal 8 Press (Lightning Originals)
An imprint of Typhoon Media Ltd

ISBN: 978-988-12196-9-5

Typhoon Media Ltd
Signal 8 Press | Distribution | Consultancy
Hong Kong
www.typhoon-media.com

Cover image: Madalena Ng (Protein Creative)

For M., for everything.

When the blackbird flew out of sight,
It marked the edge
Of one of many circles.

"Thirteen Ways of Looking at a Black Bird"
Wallace Stevens

Because quantum theory has proved infallible
in every conceivable experiment,
the same weird quantum rules must apply
to us. We, too, must exist in many states at once,
even if we don't realize it. "I don't think there
are any interpretations of quantum theory other
than many worlds. The others deny reality."

Physicist David Deutsch
Oxford, England 2001

Imagine an intersection where at the same
instant, History meets Art.
Which of these has the 'right of way'?...
Imagine an 'historical novel' set in Germany
in which German Chancellor Hitler had not
been assassinated!

Dr. Anne Frank-Koestler 1964

Contents

CHAPTER ONE

VERY little from a personal perspective has been written about the assassination of German Chancellor Adolf Hitler on July 1, 1934, following the so-called Night of the Long Knives. This night had been designated by Hilter's supporters for the arrest and elimination of Ernst Röhm and other key members of his brownshirt Stormtroopers. Because of their tactics, and particularly because the German Army could brook no challenge to its supremacy, Röhm and his Stormtrooper officers had become a political liability to the man they had helped up the ladder of power. By four p.m. on Sunday, July 1st, they were all dead.

But so was Chancellor Hitler in his Chancellery gardens.

The death of these, and of certain others to follow, brought to an abrupt end what some scholars believe could have become the most savage and inhuman era in recorded history.

The year before, in 1933, the governments of Prussia, Baden, and Bavaria rescinded all laws of the Republic against the dueling known as *Bestimmungsmensur*. The popular newspaper *Volkisher Beobachter* said, "These measures will restore the sound, healthy idea that a man should take a weapon in his hand to avenge an insult instead of going before a judge and having his honor measured by legal paragraphs, as under the Republic." Some, like priest and moral philosopher Konrad Hoeffer, felt these grudge duels were less an exercise in honor than "a resurrected ritual of pain that characterizes male puberty rites in primitive hunting societies world-wide." The subliminal purpose of this elaborate test of the male ability to endure pain, they argued, was separation from maternal identification and dominance; the role of a dubious paternity was thereby legitimized by a traumatic, second bloody birth to which adolescent males would consciously refer throughout adult life.

Contestants in the *Bestimmungsmensur* were teenagers with shaved heads. They wore narrow wire goggles to protect their eyes. A thick padded collar protected the jugular vein, and a padded sleeve protected the right arm from wrist to shoulder. A doctor, "perhaps a symbol of masculine authority," supervised the ritual, standing at a table with disinfectant, bandages, needles, and tourniquets. The doctor wiped the broad, razor-like blades of the basket-hilted rapiers to sterilize them for continued use. No real fencing went on: opponents were not to not flinch or change position. The stroke was a quick snap of the wrist. From time to time, the seconds raised their rapiers and called, "Halt!" The doctor stepped in to stanch blood and stethoscope the boys' hearts. Finally came the sewing-up of gaping cuts and the flashlight photographs to send to proud parents at home. On Chancellor Hitler's birthday in April of 1933, students at Heidelberg, celebrating in the first such duel in 547 years, sent a telegram with pledges of allegiance to their

Führer. The children of Hamlen sent a box of pretzel mice for Hitler's 44th birthday. Their card said, "You are our Pied Piper now!"

The young of Germany, especially the university students, were the Chancellor's most ardent followers and were far more anti-Semitic than either the working class or the bourgeoisie. More than ten percent of Germany was unemployed; the fragile Weimar Republic was tilting dangerously toward a communist solution. This fertile economic field was planted with seeds like Spengler's 1918 bestseller, *The Decline of the West,* in which a conflict between Civilization and Culture could only be resolved under a national ethnic-(cultural) socialist dictator. Mussolini was doing very well along these lines to the south.

*

One year later, on a mid-May afternoon in 1934, the artist's model, Lisel Ganz, so central a figure in the little-understood chain of events leading to Hitler's assassination, was coming to the corner of Gitschiner Strasse and Lindenstrasse. The warm morning sun she felt on her back put its wide hand now on her cheek. With a full stomach, she felt even the sun loved her. Her breakfast had been bought for her this morning by Horst Dörner, a corporal in the *Leibstandarte*, Hitler's contingent of one hundred personal guards. She knew the eager soldier from their hometown of Buttelstädt, a small village two hundred kilometers southwest of Berlin.

Lisel did not especially like Corporal Dörner—he was no taller than she, his nails were badly bitten down, and too much of the whites of his eyes showed when he lowered his voice to speak of things he considered terribly important. But if Lisel took exception to all the men she did not especially like, she would not eat nearly so well. Like her mother, she was at this point in her life a pragmatist.

The *Morgenpost* she saw a passing Berliner reading had the date printed too small to be seen quickly. She wondered if Horst had been right, that it was already the 12th of May. At nineteen, nearly twenty, Lisel did not keep track of the calendar much, but she had a modeling appointment for the 14th and she needed the money for a canary-yellow dress she had seen.

"Me and numbers," she had said, tapping her forehead as she sat facing Horst in the cafe where they had eaten. She had tilted her head so that loosened strands from her pinned-up, white-blond braids swept the tabletop. She had tapped her high and perfect forehead again, and closed her eyes for a moment of punctuation. It was really to wet her eyes so that when she opened them again, Horst would see them dewy. Lisel's shrug completed her helpless gesture.

She could be an actress if she really wanted to be, not just an artist's model. What was nicest about the play-acting was that it seemed to satisfy these men in Berlin. Horst "worshipped her beauty"; she was "ideal." Part of being "ideal" meant not being cornered into their beds, which was wonderful. And they bought her meals. The men Lisel knew in Berlin were mostly a boring lot. Horst had been especially boring this morning. He reminisced again about how he had gotten the scars on his cheeks. They were still a purply pink, but Horst assured Lisel that they would whiten over in time. He went on and on about the differences between scar tissue and normal skin. This, over breakfast. Lisel could gag at the thought, now that she was full.

Horst and his eye-whites and whitening scars! He had leaned over the coffee mugs and put his hand beside her own, not touching it. He had whispered, "And do you know how they sat together in a circle outside his door, all the officers, concentrating in silence together?"

She took another bite of apple from the strudel, saving the sugared crust for last. "Whose door?"

He had shaken his head tightly. "Never mind whose door, it was the circle of officers all concentrating that is the issue—"

She sipped her black coffee. "Why? What were they doing?"

He pressed his lips together; he had little patience. "They were concentrating on the man inside the office who was being interrogated. Questioned," he explained.

She tilted her head again and blinked her beautiful eyes. "I don't see the point of it at all. It sounds silly."

Horst moved his hand back to his lap. "The purpose—the purpose was to assist in the questioning process through the powers of concentration to be found in pure minds."

"Really?"

She could see by his eyes that it was. She sighed. "Forgive me. These things are all beyond me, you know. My mother had my horoscope cast one time but would never tell me what it said. And I was taken to an evening with Ursula Kardosch by an artist I model for, but I didn't follow a thing there either. I don't see why anyone would want to know what will happen beforehand, and as for knowing something especially *bad*, why suffer as much before as you must anyway after?"

"You are a philosopher after all," he said.

"You tease me."

"I adore you," he said, folding over his napkin. This was a signal that breakfast was over. She found these signals of his so boring. "As for predictions," he said in his concluding voice, "the Führer has genuine powers of prophecy. There will be a war when the State orders have been filled by industry. He has eliminated unemployment for now, but in eight years' time, he foresees there will be another economic recession. There will be only one remedy for this: the creation of more living space for our surplus population. The Western powers will never yield this vital space to us. That is why a series of decisive blows will be necessary, first in the West and then in the East."

Lisel was standing by her chair, waiting for Horst to offer her his arm to escort her out of the cafe door. "I was born during the War," she said.

"I too, in the year of its beginning." He opened the cafe door for her. Close to her, he leaned his face toward her neck and inhaled. "What a beauty you are," he whispered. She saw a tremble move through his scars. "What a beautiful womanliness, indeed."

Again he hovered close to her, and made more buzzing noises in her ear; then characteristically he withdrew with soldierly forbearance. A quick caress and a whispered "Heil Hitler" marked the end of their date. Outside, as he strode away, he turned a last time to flash a gallant smile, then he vanished around the corner.

*

Once the hideousness of his scars had faded from her mind's eye, Lisel entertained herself with the compliments that had been showered upon her. The sun on her arms as she walked past an old stone synagogue on Lindenstrasse felt like the stroking of a cat's fur, and she was the cat. Women and children came out of the temple into the brightness of Saturday morning, followed by the men. She saw them around her as colors and shapes, and the alien Hebrew sounds of a song sung by a group of children who had joined their hands above their heads were little more than a cheerful backdrop to a sunny day. As she moved around them, she smiled.

Marching in the street toward her, however, a dozen brown-uniformed men viewed her as a member of the Jewish congregation leaving the Sabbath service. Their error was understandable: like the others, she was nicely dressed (in a white suit that an older admirer had given her), and her full stomach and Horst's whispered adoration had given her face a satisfied look very similar to the religious pleasure that marked the faces of those who departed the service.

She could see by the brown of their uniforms that these approaching men were not members of Horst's elite corps; she felt her superiority wrap around her tightly like a summer shawl. It made her shift her shoulders just a bit farther back and raise her chin, as if one of the artists she modeled for had ordered a new pose. She was in no way frightened of the heavy-booted men.

But the Jews were behind her. She could feel this fear before she stopped to look at them. The mothers and fathers were calling to their children, grabbing them by the hands, and scattering as fast as they could. She looked back toward the approaching soldiers, then again at the running Jews, and something fluttered in her chest, like the fright of pigeons at a noise. The soldiers shouted. Suddenly then she was afraid, and instinctively she ran.

She had long legs, she was young, and she was frightened, but disbelief at the center of things slowed her down. It was quickly then, in an empty alley, that three of them caught her. They did not even have to knock her down. Once they had caught her, as if at tag, she stood still and waited for the game to stop. Others tackled people down the block. While she looked over her three attackers, and they her, with hard-breathing faces reddened in the May sun from the excitement and the race, she also heard various cries: of a few children as if they had fallen and skinned their knees, of mothers pleading in shrill voices, and the immediate groans of men. These sounds penetrated through the still, soft, leaf-scented perfume of the air, through the familiar surrounding vision of sidewalk, trees, and buildings that had meant Lindenstrasse only moments before. The sounds frightened her so much that her mouth was dry and she was panting; she lifted her hand to her brow.

"It's wet," she said to the three men.

They were ignoring her. It was so peculiar. She kept talking to these—one was much older, a middle-aged man, and the other two were young, about her own age. They were busy amongst themselves around her, holding her arms down, tightly—they had not liked her raising her arm to her forehead, they barked orders at her, and she obeyed; she did not know all the rules of this Berlin game. The older one who was holding her from behind, his arms pinned across her chest, had a smell of onions about him. He kept lifting his knee and jabbing her buttocks. The rough material of his pants chafed the back of her legs. The two younger ones slapped her at first, increasing in the force of the blows as a kind of match one with the other. One was reddish-haired and freckled; the other was dark, and he was growing a moustache over his lips. He was biting his lips, but the moustache was very thin.

"Dirty whore!" Onion Man screamed in her ear.

"She thinks she's better than us!" Redhair yelled. "Look at her!"

"Stop this," she ordered, surprising even herself.

"She thinks her looks fooled us!"

"Let me go this instant!" She turned, cracking her elbow across Onion Man's face. His grip momentarily loosened, then redoubled around her like a band of iron. His breathing was wild.

"Give it to her now!" he bellowed. "Now!"

"Let go!" she screamed again, when a terrible blow to her stomach caved her forward. Not a rock, it was Redhair's fist.

"Over there!" shouted Onion Man to Moustache, who bent to his left and picked up a short flat board. She screamed as the board rose above her head. Onion Man still held her; then the ground came up, a bigger, flatter, harder board. It was momentarily cushioned by the fat Onion, who rolled out from under her and threw his body down on hers. The other two stood away. Their urging cries were a kind of applause. Her vision was red.

"Jewish cunt!"

"I'm not a Jew!" she screamed. "Please!"

His breath was in her ear. "A *Mischlinge* cunt then! I'll only be screwing the Jewish half!"

She felt his first push between his stomach and hers, pushing down his pants, tearing down her white skirt, ripping down her panties. The elastic of her garters snapped against his hand and he punched her for it; she grunted against his heaving chest and tasted breakfast rising up in her throat. She vomited altogether when he stuck his prick into her; the other two laughed and laughed, but urged their fellow on for their own turns. The pain was different from the fists and board: the world was red, it smelled of blood, it was a crucifixion.

The air cooled for an instant, then another was on her, with no fumbling: he was ready, and he moved differently from the first, as if he were all of one piece, a horseman riding her. He was very quick, and his explosion seemed to blow him back from her. Her tightly closed eyes opened a slit to seem him, the Redhair. There was surprise on his face. He patted Moustache's shoulder, then shoved him toward her.

"It's easy," he muttered, "bigger and looser."

"Shut up YOUR hole!" Onion yelled. "Hurry up, the others are getting away!"

A third time her head was banged against the sidewalk, and this one used his knee to separate her thighs.

"Blood, she's bleeding," he called out.

"Never mind, it wasn't there first," one said. She could no longer, and cared no longer, to recognize each face. "Hurry up!"

This one stuck into the wet soreness and bounced above her, propping himself off her stomach and chest with his hands pressed to the cement, as if he did not want to touch her more than he had to. She was crying and blubbering Horst's name and rank and corps, but the performance above her continued, a constant rocking, each rocking a new pain.

"Oh, f'chrissakes, finish it!" one of them yelled. The voice above her head yelled back, "I can't—"

"Then put your garbage by the back door, fucker," another voice.

She could feel his relief as he quickly pulled out, slid his hands around her waist and turned her over.

"Now it looks like home!" one laughed from farther away.

She tasted the vomit again in her mouth. This pain stank as much as it split her in two. Her muscles heaved against the thrust, and all her bowels roared back. There was a new scream from above and behind, quickly followed by a firm, approving slap—amazing, she felt the sun on her skin there.

"Okay, okay, okay." She heard them dancing around her. She was lying on the sidewalk, her legs drawn up against her body painfully, but still they tucked in against the bleeding and the crampings of the muscles. The board struck her head again and again. She turned this way and that, each ear lost its hearing, and she was falling down, down and down into the cold and dark.

*

Three and a half hours later, a broad-backed man cracked the brass knocker on a wooden door on Prinzregentstrasse. The door was highly polished, extravagantly carved, and imposing. He pressed the bell and stamped on the stone step impatiently, changing the gesture as if here cleaning the bottom of his shoes so that passersby would not become suspicious. The man was out of place in this upperclass Wilmersdorf neighborhood.

Upstairs, a bell rang after the sound of knocking ceased. Albert Entrater, studiously wiping a paint brush against a soft cloth, looked around at his two friends. He was of middle height and forty years old. His looks were dark and even without being handsome. His right arm stopped at the white cuff of his shirt extending from a dark jacket. He had no right hand.

"I don't know who it is," Albert said to his friends. "I didn't even invite either of *you*."

His teasing, as usual, was met with the offhand smiles of people long accustomed to and able to see through each other's mannerisms. He smoothed the brush and laid it down beside its clean mates. He stood before a huge covered easel.

"You can never find a policeman or a housekeeper when you want one," he said. It was housekeeper Lotte's day off.

"I don't go looking for the police," Konrad said. He stood. "But I'll get the door." He sprinted out of the room and down the stairs to the main floor of the apartment.

Ludvik Brezina commented on Ludvik's exit: "He must be the Pegasus of Berlin priests." Ludvik smiled and neatly inhaled his cigarette. He was small and blond and fair, precise in all movements. Ludvik was a journalist originally from Prague. "Konrad priests as he thinks—in flying leaps. Albert, I wish I could see you actually at work. Are you mostly a mythological artist, *double entendre* thoroughly intended? All I am certain of is that you are a most accomplished cleaner of brushes!"

Albert waved him aside and moved to a chair facing the couch where Ludvik was sitting. The soft cushions of a matching chair on the other side of a large marble-mantled fireplace still kept Konrad's outline. The fireplace was dark, covered by an ornate brass fan screen.

"Don't bite the one hand that feeds you," Albert laughed.

There were double footsteps on the stairs. Konrad entered first. The man he brought with him was a startling contrast, beefy and bowed a bit at the shoulders. It seemed a habit from carrying a weight on his back, but it was as much a matter of manner as muscle. He smelled of strong beer, tobacco, and sweat. He looked around at the three faces. When he spoke, his speech had the accent of Berlin's lowest working class.

"Comrade," he addressed Albert.

"I am of all people *not* your comrade, sir."

Konrad and Ludvik laughed.

The worker nodded with his own kind of understanding, then reached into his pants pocket and drew out a name-card, Albert's. He handed it to him. Albert looked it over, front and back, saw a date he had penciled in on the back. He nodded. "And so?"

"We broke up a little brownshirt party over on Lindenstrasse a while ago. They were giving a pretty blonde a nice going-over. This is all we found on her. We carted her off to the hospital in a bad way. I didn't know how's you'd like the *polizei* connecting her name to yours, so I pocketed it."

Albert returned to his chair and sat down without offering the man a seat. He fiddled with the card. "She is my model. I expected her for this Monday." He passed the card around to verify the date. "She has posed for me twice." He looked up at the man, then seemed to see the swollen bruises on his face for the first time. He looked at the man's hands, which were also cut and bruised.

"All Nazis are bastards," Ludvik said softly.

"What is her condition?" Konrad asked the man.

"Unconscious when we carried her in. We caught the scum that got her and some of the others, I mean, some of the others who got some of the other Jews as they were coming out of the synagogue."

Konrad covered his eyes with one hand, then wiped the rest of his face down.

"She's not Jewish," Albert said. "She's one of yours, in fact, Kon."

"Will she recover?" asked Ludvik.

The man shrugged. "She was a beauty, huh? They're real brave with women and children, these shit-shirts. But that crew will be pissing blood for a while. Borman will have to dig deep in the Hilskassa kitty to patch those pigs, don't worry."

"Don't worry," Ludvik repeated with irony. "There's a rumor that they'll take a holiday from all this, all of Röhm's roughnecks. No more communist-catching and Jew-baiting for the month of July. To let the young Chancellor climb a few more rungs of his ladder, but I don't believe they can resist their fun." He started humming a popular Weill song, "Can't Help Ourselves Or You, Or Anyone."

"May the wood be old and rungs rot under Handsome Adolf's cloven feet," Konrad said. He put one finger under his nose to gesture Hitler's moustache.

"Ah, I think Goebbels could justifiably call that carping," Ludvik sneered theatrically. He referred to the Minister of Propaganda's attack the day before in the newspapers against those who found fault with the National Socialist means and ends.

"I'll be going then," the visitor said to Albert, who nodded, and walked him to the back stairs. Ludvik had stood and made as if to escort the the man out, but Albert had held up a hand to stop him.

While Albert was out of the room, Ludvik wondered what a Stormtrooper holiday would be like: "Hours of marching-band music? Boyish pranks like live burials? Sword-sharpening and bloodletting? 'You artists are limited by the civilized imagination.' Röhm and his Stormtrooper boys bathe nude in the blood-fountain of the *kultural* unconscious, if they bathe at all!"

Albert returned to the studio as Ludvik's rant flourished and died. He was putting his wallet back into his pocket and shaking his head. It was unclear whether he meant disapproval of Ludvik's comment or some commentary on his dealings with the departed visitor. As a man of means, he felt only slightly more comfortable with the communists than with the Nazis.

"Well, what is it to be, Albert?" Konrad asked.

"What is what to be?"

"We have A; now we must have B," Konrad said, mimicking Albert's familiar logical dictum. "What do you do about the girl?"

"That I do not know." Albert sat facing the priest.

Konrad went to a table where plates of bread, meat, and fruit were arranged. He bit into an apple, sniffing its scent as he chewed. "That means he's already made some arrangement. Haven't you, Albert? At least money still talks!"

Albert smiled; the back of his chair was to Konrad. "How you love to glamorize, Kon!"

"If I were an artist like you," Ludvik said by the window, "I would not paint on canvas. I would not. I would take a broad, broad brush, and refashion the whole damn world!"

"Canvas costs enough," Albert said.

"Well, I am going to the Romanisches," Ludvik announced, "despite my disdain for café crowds and revolving doors." He referred to the popular café and night-spot on Berlin's vulgar, glittery main thoroughfare.

"You can't get good conversation there either!" Albert said.

"Too true," said Ludvik.

"Tillich left Frankfurt last year," said Konrad. "And the disease has spread to Berlin."

"Hindemith, too," Ludvik added.

"Hindemith?" Albert said.

"Last week."

They had moved to the wide landing by the stairs. Ludvik put on his hat. "I had to give those Stormtroop bastards money the last time I went to Frankfurt," Ludvik complained. "I guess they don't shake you down," he said to the priest.

"Not yet," Konrad said.

"Oh, but everywhere talk is so bloody tame with everyone saying oblique goodbyes through the hat-raising and hand-shaking, you can't hear a good argument anyplace. The communists and the Nazis have taken all the good verbal violence and translated it *gutturally.*"

"Take care," said Albert to his friends. He squeezed several bills into Ludvik's hand; the young journalist made only a token resistance.

Ludvik and Konrad went down the stairs, and Albert returned to his studio and looked out the window. He gazed out at the street below and saw his friends moving away in their separate directions.

He turned from the window, walked to the large canvas, and lifted the sheet. He examined the strong-colored strokes he had added before his friends' arrival. He took some steps back, then closer again. In a characteristic gesture, he put his thumb to his mouth and bit its fullness in concentration. He strained against what he saw in the painting of myth and heard the echo of Ludvik's teasing quip. The green and gold glowed, the crimson was precisely right, but he lowered the sheet in annoyance and filled his cheeks with an exhaled sigh. He thought of Ludvik's ambition to refashion the existing world. Hard enough to *see* it, he thought. He puffed out, ran his hand down his slacks, and suddenly made for the stairs himself.

CHAPTER TWO

AFTER five days in the hospital, the girl still lay tucked in the fetal position on her side in bed. Her white room smelled of disinfectant over recently cleaned vomit. Her swollen head was bandaged whitely, so only the small delta of her bruised face showed. To Father Konrad, the bandages looked like a wimple and she looked like a beaten nun. He heard Faust roar against Mephistopheles,*"The misery of this single one pierces the marrow of my life. and you are calmly grinning at the fate of thousands!"*

She moaned, but her eyes remained swollen shut. The nurse, who was seated on the other side of the bed, stood and lifted her wrist to feel her pulse. Konrad watched her face register the information as the nurse looked at a watch attached to the belt of her uniform.

"It's well up beyond sixty," she said, nodding. "I must get the doctor."

He could tell by her tone that it was good news. He leaned toward the bed after the nurse had left the private room, and he called the girl's name.

Small slits appeared in her face; she strained to open her eyes.

"I am a priest," he said.

"Am I dying?" she whispered.

We are all, he thought. *Living* is *dying*. By the time he shook off his self-absorption, she was again unconscious. Often now, he so thoroughly disliked himself. *Better naturalist and astronomer than priest*, he thought. The door opened and he expected to see the nurse return with the doctor.

Instead, in the doorway stood a stark figure in a black uniform marked with red and metal. He thought of the black blister beetle with its yellow-and-red markings, distant cousin to the more familiar firefly. The soldier introduced himself as Corporal Dörner, one of Chancellor Hitler's personal guards.

The effect was something out of a silent movie comedy because the head snapping and the heel clicking were soundless. The priest knew the fatigue of his two-day vigil was making him giddy, but there was something about these Nazis that made him feel like laughing. It reminded him of the feeling he had had as a child when guilty friends were punished by their parents in his presence. He stifled the anxious laughter in his throat.

Horst walked close to the bed, looked down at the girl and whispered a curse. Then, more audibly, he added, "This is the work of communists and their Jew money."

"I believe it was a gang of brownshirts who attacked the girl," the priest said.

"It is not a revolution of bourgeois shopkeepers the Stormtroopers are about."

Konrad nodded. "Nevertheless." Then he smiled.

Horst did not know if the priest was mocking him or

not. He turned from him and stared down at the girl, who was curled up with her back to him.

"The important point is that she is better," Konrad said. "The nurse only just left."

"Yes?" The Nazi looked hopeful. It was the first time Konrad could see anything recognizable in the young man's face. The door opened again, and this time the nurse did enter with an elderly doctor. Horst took several steps back to allow the doctor to examine the patient.

When the doctor touched her wrist, she groaned. The doctor nodded to the nurse, who smiled. Konrad saw the slits of Lisel's eyes open again.

"What is it? What is it?" she began crying, first in a whisper, then in a strengthening voice that rose to a scream. "No!"

She pushed off the doctor's hand and pushed with both her hands against the empty air. The exertion pained and exhausted her, and she fell back from the strain, whimpering.

The nurse leaned over her, to calm her and smooth her sheet and blanket. But her closeness seemed only to distress Lisel more.

"Gloves… in back... of drawer!" she cried.

She opened her eyes, trying to focus them. The doctor ordered a sedative; he had to repeat the order to the nurse, who was looking at Lisel oddly. Then the nurse seemed to shake herself and promptly left the room. The doctor looked about, at the priest, then at the soldier, then at the bureau Konrad stood near. On the bureau was a vase of many-colored gladioli, a box of chocolates, and a blue dish of grapes. In the bottom drawer the doctor found a forgotten pair of gloves, left behind by a patient who had died in the his care six months earlier.

"Interesting case," the doctor said.

"Herr Doctor—" Horst began.

"Time," the doctor interrupted with the familiar answer. "It will surely take time and bedrest." He attempted to lean over Lisel again, now that she breathed regularly. He touched her swollen eyelid with a delicacy Konrad admired, and began to shine a pencil light into her eyes.

It was as if a trapped bird hid in the cave of her mind. She screamed again, this time at the doctor: "October, she'll be dead!"

The medical man drew back, glanced quickly around, and pocketed the pencil light. Avoiding Konrad's curious gaze, he spoke to her: "Calm yourself now, young lady. There is nothing more to fear." There was a tremor in his voice, which he had tried to force down to its lowest, most professional register.

The nurse returned, but the doctor waved away the syringe she offered him on a tray. Instead, he demanded the patient's chart, and, receiving it, wrote for several moments. Then without another word, he left the room. The nurse looked down at the chart.

"What is it?" Horst said.

The nurse hesitated and looked at Konrad, who only tilted his head. Horst took a step toward the nurse, and she, along with Konrad, did not doubt the young officer would take the chart from her hands. Instead of relinquishing her medical authority, however, she gathered herself together and looked down at the chart, as if for the first time.

"Psychiatric," she announced. She nodded as if agreeing with the doctor's determination; then she too left the room.

Horst and Konrad faced one another across the white bed. The priest felt he could not leave the girl alone with this Nazi, although he also felt distinctly that this was what was wanted. Then, surprisingly, the young officer knelt in the position of prayer, and this action so moved Konrad that he felt like placing a hand on the penitent's short blond hair to bless him. Horst held still for some time, then rested his head against Lisel's back that held strictly to the edge of the bed. At his touch, she moaned again, deeply.

"Sweetheart," he echoed her moan.

The priest was drawn towards Lisel, and leaned toward her struggling face. He bent down so that his head was beside her lips to hear what she was whispering. To Horst, on the other side of the bed, it was no more than choking breathing. He was at the ready to spring and run for the doctor.

"Hummingbird," she whispered again and again.

Colibri the word automatically translated in Konrad's mind (*Colibri*!). He was about to stroke the suffering girl's shoulder when he grasped the effect touch had on her. He stood again. Horst stood with him, assuming his rigid self-control.

"She needs rest, the doctor said," Horst ordered himself, snapping his head down and up at his own command. Acknowledging the priest briefly, he turned on his heel and left the room.

Konrad sat down on the chair by the window. He felt the warm sun through the glass-like hands rubbing his tired shoulders. Automatically, he folded his hands and prayed inwardly, allowing himself the luxury of the thought that Albert would come once it was dark, and this night he might be able to go to bed and sleep, though sleep for months had been a stranger to him.

"Be with us now and in the hour of our death. Amen," he prayed in silence.

"Be with us now and in the hour of our death. Amen," her whispers echoed his thought exactly.

Some hours later, she opened her eyes and tried to focus in the dark. She could tell, she did not know how, that the nurse and priest were not in the room with her, but she was not alone. She heard hospital sounds outside her door. She heard metal and wheels and quickly moving feet. She felt in her body for pain, but it was hiding in particular places now. It was no longer everywhere. Her head hurt the worst, but still not so bad as before. It did not pound with her pulse, and the terrible nausea was gone. Where she was raw and hot and sore she did not like to think about. Her eyes focused in the dark from the streetlight coming up into the window. Her hand fluttered to her head in confusion. Searching, she felt the stiff edges of bandages. A man was standing by the window looking up at the night sky.

"Father?" she said.

The figure turned. "No. It is Herr Entrater. How are you feeling?"

"Herr Entrater?"

"Yes. Do you want anything?" Albert asked, uncomfortably.

"Where is my hair!" she cried. "They cut off my hair!"

"Ssh," he soothed.

"I want to go home! Please!"

"All right now, you must try to go back to sleep, Lisel. You must rest yourself."

Herr Entrater had a foolish high voice, but sweet, and he began to tell her a story as if she were a little girl: *"Once many, many years ago, seven sisters went walking, and one became lost in the forest. One of the seven brothers in the Big Dipper found her, and her beauty was such that he fell in love with her at once…"*

As she listened to the story, she stopped crying. Then slowly she untucked her legs and stretched them out under the sheet and blanket. It was cool against her calves and bare feet. She let herself sink into the softening mattress, into the echo of the sound of his voice.

CHAPTER THREE

TWO weeks later, on May 25th, little more than a month before the assassination of German Chancellor Hitler, the enclosed gardens of Albert Entrater above the Prinzregentstrasse were thriving. Trees in full flower, some already dropping their clusters, had gone fully into green leaf. Tulips and daffodils crowded the banks of well-tended earth around the trees. Roses were also in full bud by this early Friday evening, and the pachysandra was white with flower. The mix of floral perfumes rose into the wide window of the dining room and onto the apartment's main floor, a large, modern architected space used for entertaining. This floor showed a marked difference from the studio-salon and bedrooms upstairs, for the public Albert Entrater was a man of the modern world of art and ideas. The private man—the part-Jew (*Mischlinge*), the artist—this man lived and worked in a museum of memories. There was a striking contrast as well between the setting in which he worked and the paintings he produced, some of which hung on the enormous white walls of the main floor.

These large mythological and surreal scenes and one of the many gilt-framed triptychs by which he was often characterized were completely upstaged this evening by the colors of the forbidden German flag, worn by every guest to a most unusual party. Everyone, including the band, was wearing black, red, and gold to protest the book burnings of 1933, when gangs of Nazis and Nazi sympathizers had conducted the announced and carefully planned fiery purge of non-Aryan intellectual imperfection.

The men this evening were more likely to be wearing red and yellow ties and black slacks, and the women, more flamboyantly, wore flowing scarves and painted shoes—many were artists like the men. The musicians had been provided with the tricolor at the door, handkerchiefs knotted together now stuck in their black jacket breast pockets; in fact, a flash of gold-red-black usually meant that one of the trumpet players had found a rest in which to mop his brow with his festive party favor.

The bass player, when the spirit moved him, sang lyrics of the songs he played. The guests closest to the band listened appreciatively, but the busy waiters under the watchful eye of housekeeper Lotte ignored the paintings on the walls, the flag-costumed guests, and focused their eyes on the silver salvers of hors d'oeurvres and cocktails. Liquor threatened to run over the crystal cups of the guests as they listened and swayed to the slapping jazz drums, the muted and then wailing trumpets, the bass's throb as its player sang a currently popular tune from America.

The bassist looked up, his white face and hungry eyes surprised and pleased at the attention he was getting. A woman leaned her cocktail glass to his lips, and he sipped. Then she, along with several others, sang with the bassist. All the voices joined in for the end of the song, as people at the edge of the group danced a few ballroom steps and the song became contagious throughout the room, rippling over it like rising water. There was a burst of applause and laughter that ebbed slowly.

Ludvik watched the lively scene disperse as he stood beside his host, who was, he noted, characteristically somber. Indeed, in the last several weeks, the last two in particular, Albert had felt himself becoming unsettled. His involvement on behalf of this girl he barely knew, and also now in the last two weeks Konrad's sudden disappearances: each of these contributed to a growing state of unease. Particularly, there was the girl, he thought; about her there was something truly unnerving. His brow was wrinkled and his eyes darted around the room. Konrad had been inexplicably "tied up" at the last moment.

"Are you still tired from the trip to the boonies?" the Czech asked Albert. He referred to the journey his host had made with Lisel to her family home to the south.

"I don't dream of returning to Buttelstädt in this lifetime, if that's what you mean," Albert answered, intending to brighten.

"Did you leave her there?"

"Yes."

The band was playing a melancholy cabaret tune.

"Perhaps your idea for this party played better over the wine and wurst," Ludvik said after a pause.

"Where is the Hungarian, anyway?" Albert changed the subject.

Understanding, Ludvik answered as idly, "I don't know.

They are always unpredictable—maybe he'll show up later with the new girlfriend."

Across the room, a little bald-headed man was denouncing Stormtroop leader Ernst Röhm. He punctuated his presentation with obscenities and facial contortions, particularly of his mouth and tongue, which was red and darted forth like an adder's.

"The Hungarian doesn't like to go out at night anymore, I think," Albert said.

"Of course, it can be dangerous," Ludvik replied.

The denouncer had mounted a table and was now reeling off a full list of Nazi villains, for each of which he provided a disparaging epigram that produced howls of appreciative laughter. Albert was clearly ill at ease with the performance, and his nervousness annoyed Ludvik who was enjoying the show.

"Relax, Albert," he chided. "The Nazis can't afford your neighborhood, and even if they could, we might all say we're *celebrating* book-burning rather than repudiating it."

"No doubt," the host said without the slightest conviction, then looked away in the direction of the foyer, out of his view, where there was a table piled high with the kind of books the Nazis had chosen for burning the year before. Aside from the center-ring performance, guests all around the large room were exchanging and discussing these and other books with great eschatological energy. Of course, Ludvik was right, Albert thought; there was no clear and present cause for his anxiety. Inside him nonetheless the uneasy feeling had taken root, and its leaves rustled with the faintest breeze. The little bald man finished his presentation. with a comical goosestep that was extremely funny, even Albert admitted, and he marched off to the dinner table with a number of chattering friends.

"Did you get the *Murder in Three Acts* I sent?" Ludvik asked.

"Yes." Albert nodded and smiled. It pleased Ludvik. "I love it. Mrs. Christie is extraordinarily clever in this one."

"And possibly prescient. Did you notice the similarities?"

A grey-haired artist with Parkinson's walked across the floor. His jittery walk went well with the now raucously welcomed jazz again being played. He joined his friends with a stein of beer filled to overflowing in his hand. As Ludvik and Albert continued to talk about the Agatha Christie novel, the man drank deeply from the beer, emerging from each swallow with a new foamy moustache he licked away with appreciative tongue, like a ship in heavy seas plunging into and out of great foamy waves. What brew didn't reach his mouth fell in great splashes onto the shiny wooden floor. He was soon standing in his own small pool of beer.

"And let me also thank you for that Niebuhr book you managed for me," Ludvik said.

"But is the man a *theologian*?" Albert replied, and Ludvik laughed heartily at the imitation of Konrad's irritation.

"Where is Konrad, by the way?"

"Nowadays, I don't know."

"Words, words!" the afflicted artist gestured wildly as he joined Albert and Ludvik, nearly overturning a silver tray a waiter was carrying by.

"Give me brushes and paint and someone who'll buy Jew art!"

Ludvik pointed to the baldheaded performer. "I think he's crazy!"

"Ha! Half the stuff he stole from me! No. I mean it, that remark about little Adolf, for instance—I said that to him last month in this very room. You remember that, Albert."

"I think I do."

"The remark about the *boots*."

"Yes. I seem to recall."

"That remark about the boots was *entirely* of my *own* invention. And the remark about Granniger, the Nazis' pimp."

"Why is it *I* never hear these comical remarks from you?"

"I am not disposed to be comical in your presence, Ludvik."

"I see."

"Czechs are not known for the appreciation of the comical side of life."

"But I've appreciated *you* for ten years!"

"There! That is Czech humor at its wittiest."

"And Austrian humor, your own?"

"The grandest joke of all is Austrian, my friend. Currently he resides at the Chancellery!" the man triumphed shakily.

A woman walking near them held a thick book against her chest with one arm; in her other hand she held a thick cigarette from which she inhaled for emphasis.

"*Barbarians*!" she announced to the trio, too loudly.

"Barbarians worship fire! First the Reichstag fire, now—! First, the laws, then the books, the literature of *the civilized world*!" She paused for breath, coughed, inhaled from her cigarette deeply, and exhaled clouds of smoke through her nose and mouth that created a ring of cloud. The shaking man blew the smoke back at her. Glaring at him, she quoted Goebbels with great irony, "Oh century, it is a joy to live!" The artist coughed in response. She nodded to Ludvik, looked about as if for an ashtray, and apparently locating one, vanished as quickly as she appeared.

"Do you know her?" Albert asked.

"Her husband was the literary critic at the paper. Up until they fired all of us. The only thing she read till then was tea leaves. Now she's a defender of literary art!"

There was a general deflation at Ludvik's allusion to the Nazi "purchase" in April of Germany's most respected newspaper, *Vossische Zeitung*. Ludvik had been an editor there until the previous October when an edict ordered that all editors must be Aryan.

Without being noticed, the servants had turned lights on in the wide, white room, as night overtook twilight. Those standing talking by the windows would, if inclined to look out, have seen the streetlamps assume their electric imitation glow of gaslamps of an earlier era. In Berlin's many parks, fireflies twinkled in the dark grass like stars more easily viewed away from city lights. If observers had looked at the southeastern sky, beyond the brightness of Jupiter, they would have also seen Mars closest to Saturn. The ironic conjunction of these planets echoed the band's disharmonious playing; for here was Saturn, his reign considered a Golden Age, celebrated around what was in the modern age Christmastime, next to Mars, the Roman god of war. In late May, the one planet was paradoxically poised close to the other, though in Konrad's absence there was no one besides Albert to notice such celestial commentary.

Ludvik showed a bluebound playscript to his friends. "I saw this in Paris last month. I'm writing about it now. It's Cocteau's version of *Oedipus* and funny, considering it is French, and he has our Adolf on his mind, too."

"He is not *my* Adolf," the shaking man grumbled.

Ludvik shook his head. "In any case," he looked at Albert, "in Oedipus we have the *original* motherfucker, yes!"

Albert smiled. The other let it sink in slowly like salve, then laughed.

"Is this Cocteau's view or yours?" Albert asked.

Ludvik was delighted. "Well, you know the French. They are in reality no better than cowardly Germans! Here, listen to this, you'll get the idea." Ludvik had found the place he looked for in the script.

"Yes. A mother is talking about her sons who are always fighting. She says that they cannot live together under the same roof. Now the one who's sixteen is only interested in politics. He says the Sphinx is a *hoax*. There *might* have been a Sphinx at one time according to him, but now this Sphinx is now *dead*, so the priests use it as a *bogey* to scare the people, and the police use it as a *cover-up* for their inefficiency and corruption. In Thebes, there is starvation, rising prices, bandits infesting the countryside, no government to speak of, one bankruptcy after another—why? The Sphinx! The temples are crammed with holy offerings, while mothers with families haven't a loaf of bread to call their own. Wealthy tourists are leaving the city—"

"*And* the Jews!"

"'And why?" Ludvik continued with a nod to the shaking man. "It is because of the Sphinx. And then the mother says," Ludvik read, gesturing, "'He gets up on the table, this sixteen-year-old boy, shouting and waving and stamping, denouncing the authorities, preaching revolution and praising the anarchists. What we need,' says his *mother*, 'what we need is a *man*, an *iron fist*, a *dictator*!'" Ludvik looked up, his pale face flushed, his eyes bright.

"It's a healthy thing for Cocteau he's in Paris," Albert said. He took the playscript from Ludvik's hand. He leafed through it, expertly cradling it in his right arm, not reading, merely turning pages with his left.

"But we never do get it right, do we?" he added. "I wonder where we get the—"

"—*Chutzpah*?" Ludvik teased.

"—to keep trying. Perhaps," he ignored Ludvik's Yiddish, waving the script to imply the roomful of guests, "the same place *they* get the *nerve* to come here for a party like this."

"They? You invited everyone," Ludvik said.

"Oh, no. I am only the occasion of sin, as Konrad would say. You have all exercised free will in coming here."

Ludvik looked at Albert oddly. "Why do you do that?"

"Do what? "

"Disengage yourself."

"He was born to it," the shaking man said. "Look about you, see? This is Albert's domain. As the world crumbles around him, he paints his triptychs, and you and I, Ludvik, and all the rest are to him mere daubs of oil paint."

"Your excess eludes me, my friend," Albert said.

"Your moderation smothers me!"

"We turn on each other," Ludvik protested.

The shaking man found himself by the end of this last remark so aggrieved that he turned away and stumbled to the dinnertable. Ludvik stayed silently beside Albert for a while, then took the script gently back from his hand, lightly touched Albert's right forearm, and led him over to join in the dinner. Well into the night, the guests talked about the many books that across the city fueled a mounting blaze. It was the last party Albert was to give in Berlin.

Hours later, after all the revelers had departed, Albert sat with Konrad, who had arrived only in time for port and cigars. Konrad had a plate of dinner and a bottle of wine beside him on the table by his chair. He had his feet up on a soft ottoman. He ate with a hunger slowed by obvious fatigue.

"Was it such a disagreeable party, then?" he asked.

The night air moved like a ghost around the two men.

"His illness upsets me. My wealth irritates him."

Konrad watched Albert as he sank back into his club chair, thumb-tip in his mouth. He was biting with some concentration.

"Parkinson's is a disease of the nerves."

"Both kinds," Albert said.

Konrad found another slice of meat. "Our friend is our homeland in miniature."

"Everyone confides in you."

"I am a priest," he smiled. He sipped his wine.

"We missed you tonight."

"I am sorry. I was obliged to be elsewhere."

"Yes." Albert waited, but nothing was added. He filled his glass with wine. "My brother has written me. He is also afraid. He analyzes our situation at length."

"Dear Artur. How is he?"

"He is well."

"Living in New York?"

"Yes."

Konrad refilled his own glass.

"His letter has made me think. We don't belong to the West, despite our pretenses; we don't have the spirit for democracy like the English... in fact, I think more and more as Joseph Conrad said, we have at best the spirit of cynicism."

"I believe Conrad was referring to the *Russians* when he wrote that," Konrad observed.

"It applies as well to us."

"Perhaps you're right."

"The point is," he paused, "The point is, this cannot be stopped, can it?

"*This*... the paper-hanger?"

"Yes."

Konrad shook his head. "We are even afraid to use his

name now. He has become such a god, his name is forbidden to our mouths. The facts in the case are unique. There are two and a half million of Röhm's Stormtroopers like the scum who attacked the girl, and there is also the paper-hanger. So we have a scorpion with two stingers, a freak of nature. Can it be stopped? Notice also: we use the *passive* voice: 'Can it be stopped?' Can it be stopped by *whom*?"

Albert rose and turned. "I was out there, outside the 'walls' of Berlin... in the country it is different."

"In Buttelstädt?"

"Yes."

"Albert?" said the priest quietly.

"Permit me… I ramble, I know, but permit me. First, there is Einstein. Yes? And Bruno Walter. And Mann on the boat to New York this very moment. And Toscanini. And Klemperer beaten. Just like the girl."

Konrad looked down at his folded hands. The sound of the confessional voice was familiar to him, although unique from his boyhood friend.

"And then there are people—in Buttelstädt—people whose faces are empty, *faceless*—" Albert stopped, squinted, seeing something in memory. "On the road there was a sign: 'Dangerous Curve! Slow Down! Jews Excepted!'"

The air in the large room was still.

"My money," he began again, "was out of the country before the '31 tax law', but for how long can any come back in? And my God, shouldn't the fascists be more friendly to capitalists than communists? Why is my hand always in my pockets for the wrong side?" His voice settled to a conclusion. "I have observed something: cities are *not* countries. Whoever got people to think of themselves as countrymen? We are just *Berliners*, you and I. We are *not* Germans, *none* of us!"

"Albert," Konrad said calmly.

"Do I make sense?"

The priest sighed. "Yes," he nodded. He was familiar with his friend's excess of emotion, especially his sudden dark certainties. "Yes, you make sense." He smiled. "Generally speaking, you always make sense."

"Thank you."

"Generally speaking." He winked.

"But? "

"But matters are no worse than they were last week." An intuition whispered in the priest's ear and he spoke softly. "So tell me what happened to you in Buttelstädt."

"Why?"

"Tell me."

Albert twisted under the question. "I took her to her mother. I walked around the town. I went to the church."

"The girl?"

"Yes."

"And?

He paused. "And she 'sees' things. Like looking through walls. I had to argue with her mother, a witch, to keep her there."

"And so she scared you, the girl?"

He nodded.

"You believe she can see the future?"

"I don't know. You heard her in the hospital. She looks like she's been hit by a gust of wind. When she calms, she sorts it out, but there's no time to it, no limit of distance."

Konrad nodded. "It's fascinating, if true."

"I saw her. I heard."

"And what did she see?"

"She saw me."

"How?

"She saw me dead in a charnel house."

Konrad, distracted, finished his drink. "All right, old friend, now listen to me."

"Konrad," Albert interrupted and spoke quickly. "Don't get your fingers caught in the machinery of state, or you will never—"

"Never what?"

He paused. "I don't know. I'm not sure."

"Are you also hearing voices?"

"No. Of course not."

"Has this girl had a vision?"

"I don't know." Albert shook his head. "I feel uneasy. I am so very deeply uneasy."

Konrad rose from the soft chair. He spoke quietly. "The girl is charismatic—"

"Kon—"

"But clairvoyant, that's another matter—"

"Where have you been going?"

Another pause.

"I have been meeting with colleagues."

"What colleagues?"

Konrad went to the open window. He breathed in the night air. He looked up and saw south of the Dipper, Saturn, and Mars brighter than Spica and Virgo.

"I will tell you something, Albert," he said, still looking out. "There is a thesis I am coming to grasp. A group of us have become intrigued by the problem. The implications are enormous." He turned.

"What is this *thesis*?"

The look of distress that flashed across Albert's face was signal enough; the priest knew his old friend had neither the training nor the temperament to hear the confession he had almost begun. The Devil's death would remain a matter of his own concern. The Devil's dark face fluttered before him now, as it had since the visits to the white room in the hospital just two weeks (was it a lifetime?) ago. In the distance, the voice of his old companion rose and fell. He listened and made replies.

"A group of colleagues like myself. Oddballs, actually..."

How many futures are there, he thought. How many versions of the Plot? What had the girl *seen*? What did the girl know?

CHAPTER FOUR

A week later, on June 7th, in the evening's newspapers throughout Germany, Stormtrooper Chief Ernst Röhm made official the announcement that Ludvik Brezina had heard rumored:

I have decided to follow the advice of my doctors and take a cure in order to restore my energies which have been severely strained by a painful nervous complaint. My place will be taken by the Chief of the Leadership Office, Obergruppenführer von Krausser.

1934 will require all the energies of every Stormtroop fighter. I recommend, therefore, to all Stormtroop leaders to begin organizing leave early in June.

Therefore, for a limited number of Stormtroop leaders and men, June, and for the majority of Stormtroops, July, will be a period of complete relaxation in which they can recover their strength.

I expect the Stormtroops to return on 1 August completely rested and refreshed in order to serve in those honourable capacities which nation and fatherland expect of them. If the enemies of the Stormtroops live in hope that the Stormtroops will not return, or will return only in part, from their leave, we will allow them this brief pleasurable anticipation. They will receive the appropriate reply at the time and in the manner most suitable.

The Stormtroops are and remain Germany's destiny."

*

Two days later, Lisel sat very still in the cab seat of the truck two hundred kilometers south of Berlin. She was so upset she did not see or hear anything Horst's uncle said; he was driving her to Weimar for the train back to Berlin. Two weeks at home had made her strong enough to leave, and she knew her mother had desperately wanted her to go.

When Lisel was upset, she did not feel the hot waves, like water, break against her from people who touched her, or brushed past her, or who put a coffee cup in her hand. Her hands were folded tightly in her lap in Horst's truck. The sixty-year-old man was none too happy to be driving her, but Horst had called all the way from Berlin and said that Lisel's wishes were to be obeyed. Uncle Karl could give orders to Horst's mother, his sister, but he had to take them from his nephew.

As Uncle Karl drove through the fertile countryside, he told himself the good of it was a Saturday spent doing something he could tell about later over a stein in the beer-hall in Buttelstädt. He would say (he rehearsed in his mind as he avoided a dog on the road), "The departure of a looney from Buttelstädt is an event; the arrival of a looney in Berlin is *history*!" Uncle Karl smiled to himself at his cleverness and the approval his friends would show him. They said he had wasted his talents as a farmer, he should have been a writer with his wit. But he said, "It's better to grow food people can eat than write books they have to burn!" Everyone took it as proof of his cleverness.

"No. Stop!" Lisel said.

"What is it?" Uncle Karl asked. He kept his voice kind, for Horst's sake. He was also somewhat afraid of the girl's new strangeness. She had always been merely a very pretty, simple girl from a poor family, father dead in the Great War, an object of pity, not fear, until now.

"Not south," she said. "Please drive north."

He tightened his hands on the steering wheel. Who was paying for the gasoline for all this? Horst? Ha! The look on the girl's face, however, convinced him to turn the truck around. "Back home?" he said, trying to sound understanding.

"No," she commanded. She would suit Horst, after all. "Just north, the road to Sommerda. I went there with Mr. Entrater."

He obeyed, shaking his head all the way.

"There's nothing here," he said along the narrow country road.

A dense crowding of young beech trees shaded their route. Behind the young trees there were bigger trees where loud insects and birds argued over territory on the fine spring day. The air was filled with sweetness of wildflowers and wet earth. Uncle Karl breathed in, sticking his head out the truck window. In the unseen distance was the stump of an ancient oak that the poet Goethe was supposed to have often sought out.

"That's no farm smell," he sniffed. "It's just the bees making honey."

She tried to smile, but the feeling was coming on her like dark clouds. She looked out the window. The sky was high and blue, and the only clouds were the fat lambkin kind that one would watch change shapes in the wind.

She seemed to see through the blue sky, through the plump clouds, as if they were a curtain on a stage gone transparent from stage lighting. Behind the painted sky it was dark and deep, cave-like. It was cold, and Lisel shivered.

"Stop," she whispered hoarsely. Then more loudly, "Stop!"

"Oh—" Uncle Karl swallowed a curse. "We're in the middle of nowhere, Lisel."

"I have to get out," she whimpered.

He drew over to the side of the road. It was midday. He pulled the truck emergency brake and watched her open the door, jump down from the cab, and run through the young trees into the woods as if drawn jerkily on a string like a marionette. He tried to believe she had to take a leak or maybe had the runs, but she gave him the chills. He relaxed when she was gone. He was glad, like an anvil had been taken out of the seat that had been tilting the ride, wearing down the front left tire on her side. He took off his black cloth cap and ran his fingers through his damp hair. It was a warm day; now that she was gone, he felt the heat.

She whimpered all the way through the trees, slipping on mushrooms that had grown up overnight in the wet. She had hoped the other time, with Mr. Entrater, driving south from Sommerda where he said, he said? he said his *wife's family*—but she was dead, and Lisel knew there had been a child, a daughter, three or four years old; she had *seen* her—Lisel had hoped the other time it was the beating that had brought on the strangeness. The horrible sight.

"Weimar," she said out loud, trying to break the spell. She could have been in Weimar by now, sitting on a wooden bench at the train station. Instead, she stood in a column of sunshine facing a silvery beech. A robin flew past her sight, a blur of orange-brown.

Beyond the beech she could feel like gusts of a breeze the open, unbroken field. She could see what she would see if she took only a few more steps—pointed wire, a windswept hill flattened by many feet, striped cloth grey and white and yellow stars. A galaxy of yellow stars. There was the *smell* again in the air, of burning feathers. She felt dizzy; her tongue gagged the back of her mouth; she reached out to steady herself against the beech—it was smooth against her palm.

"What is the matter?" Uncle Karl said behind her, out of breath. She turned to stare at him but the light fell through the trees in a strange way, and she could not see the man clearly. She frowned.

"You screamed—what is wrong?"

She turned and pointed towards the low and run-down buildings only she could see.

"You're nuts," he said. He moved to reach her extended hand and lead her back to the truck.

"No, look!" she said fiercly, grasping his thick hand first

and pulling him with uncanny strength. She pulled him several steps till he trotted alongside her curiously. They reached an opening in the woods, and the girl's blue eyes opened wide as saucers as she stared at a grassy flat rimmed with dark trees. She put up both her hands to hold off a wall about to fall on her. "*NO*!" she screamed.

She felt him catch her as she fell, but when she turned to look into his face, it had changed horribly, first into a black cloud electric with blue and white sparks, then into a hollowed skull-face, the same face she had seen before. She squeezed her eyes shut, but could still smell the stink of burning feathers rising off his charred body. Then, mercifully, nothing.

Uncle Karl lifted the unconscious girl easily, and he thought of what he had heard the three Berliners had done. If it came to it, he was now ready to ride the train with her all the way to Berlin. Everybody knew the mother didn't want her anymore; she thought the girl was a devil. Perhaps she was right. If so, then goddammit, he felt pity for the devil.

There was only a small village nearby. Could he find a doctor there somewhere in Buchenwald?

CHAPTER FIVE

LISEL arrived at Albert's door brought by the old farmer on the following day. The village doctor had recommended hot baths and hypnosis, which his own wife in menopause had found helpful. Uncle Karl recognized a quack when he saw one and hurried the girl away. The Buchenwald doctor had also suspected, though he never said it, that the girl was pregnant. It was only intuition on his part, but he had for some time prided himself on recognizing the invisible manifestations of hidden life; in fact, he was composing a particularly interesting treatise on the topic which a series of publishers would later reject out of hand.

To Albert, the pair on his doorstep was a portrait in itself. It had been five weeks since the girl had been attacked, three weeks since he had taken her to Buttelstädt. Since then, the bruises on her face had become shadows or shades of yellow, and now in her blue eyes was a fiery flickering. How to sketch that? The tense focus-refocusing of those eyes? But her fine jaw was now more accessible, outlined by the short curve of hair that cupped her perfect cheeks. Her hair was still that remarkable white-blonde that drew the hand to touch it, but it was bruised in its own way by the cutting.

"She can't stay alone," the old farmer grunted, clutching his cap. "Can she stay with you? She says it's quiet here."

"Yes," he heard himself say. "Yes, of course." He saw her grateful eyes. "Lotte," he called as the farmer left, but Lotte was at the market. Maintaining his sense of authority, he escorted the girl to one of the extra rooms upstairs and left her there to rest until dinner at which she barely spoke despite his coaxing. The true understanding of her arrival came to him later that night.

It had been another warm day, part of the unnatural weather. Yet Lisel complained of the cold, and he had covered her with whatever he could find that Lotte had not stored away for the summer. One of the coverings was an old forgotten sweater of Konrad's. Soon after she had fallen asleep, she began to move under it, and her eyes darted back and forth under her closed lids. He was just outside the bedroom when she cried out.

He rushed in and she repeated the outcry of Konrad's name. He was transfixed by her writhing and cries, now an incantation. She was still sound asleep, of that he was certain; and when he reached down to her, he felt the damp chill she had complained of—it was the same as the time of her seizure in the Buchenwald area near Buttelstädt.

Albert wakened Lisel as gently as he could, but she shuddered. She opened her eyes but didn't see him. She startled him when she seized his hand, vise-like, between her fisted palms.

"He has nothing to do with it!" she insisted as if she were testifying. Her hands were damp and cold.

"Who? What?" he asked. "You are only dreaming. It is only a dream."

She looked at him, wetted her dry lips with her tongue. Holding Albert's hand had calmed her. Her quick breathing began to slow.

"Only like this with you it is quiet." Lisel took several slow, deep breaths. "Otherwise, the world is screaming, pushing at me. I feel so hollow." She sighed like wind blowing through a reed.

He felt her cool hand open and clutch his, and felt a pang in his phantom right arm. The fear he had first experienced with her on the road to Buttelstädt had subsided somewhat, but now once again, her emotions entered him like an electric current.

"What's it like?" Lisel whispered, looking at his cropped arm. She pulled him down so he sat on the edge of the bed.

He shook his head.

"It's not *like* anything. Primary colors are themselves."

She waited for more. Like a child.

"I felt nothing when it was blown off." He saw light and a fierce gust of wind knocking him down. "It hurt after, when they cleaned it and bandaged it. I screamed but I could not faint."

She was a child after all, only nineteen, only a young girl.

"Sometimes," he continued, "when I must use the left hand, I feel like I am in the wrong body, as you say, hollow."

"We are soul-mates then," she smiled.

"In a sense."

"I am so tired."

"Then you must sleep."

"Yes."

Her grip began to loosen, and soon she had fallen back asleep. At once he was reminded how a small child's hands are fists until she sleeps deeply. Then, the little hands open into the vulnerable flowers of their palms.

Albert rose, he wondering what Lisel had seen of Konrad, for he now believed that she had seen him though he had no sense as yet of what her *visions* meant. She was not, he was certain, insane; he could not prove this. It was an assertion, a major proposition derived from an inexplicable syllogism of faith. All of us were dependent on faith of some sort, even the atheists; we depend upon it to get from one day to the next. He comforted himself with this old thought—which was also an assertion of faith!

But then perhaps he was losing his grip. Ludvik had once said, "You put a crazy into a room full of sane men, and it is they who will question their sanity and go mad." The crazy room of Germany had been the target of Ludvik's observation, Hitler the source of madness. Maybe the girl had chosen to make Albert's home her asylum.

He went out of the house for a breath of air. It was summer, and the twilight was a good long time, crowded with ardent fireflies like stars twinkling in the grass.

CHAPTER SIX

WITHIN the week, German Chancellor Hitler was in Venice with Mussolini for the state visit of June 14. Appropriately, the Italian leader would be the only foreign statesman at the Chancellor's funeral three weeks later.

Albert was also at work, re-examining the three large canvas panels of his triptych, looking from them to the sheets of sketches clipped to adjoining easels. He had lifted his brush from the left panel, a scene from *The Nibelungeleid* of the betrayal by a river, when Hagen murdered Seigfried.

The middle panel was blocked out in wash on the canvas and was detailed in the pen-and-ink sketches on its corresponding easel. This was a modern street in Berlin. A baton-wielding conductor was being overpowered, beaten to the ground by the brownshirted Stormtroopers swinging baton-like black twisted iron crosses.

The last panel and sketches-on-easel were still a surprise to Albert. Following Lisel's arrival, it had come to mind whole, insisting itself into being. When he looked at the sketches, he could feel in his stomach the compulsion that had run along the nerves of his body, pressing hard through the fingers of his left hand, resulting in painful cramp. It was the stark scene "The Hanging of Haman" from the Book of Esther.

Mordecai, Esther's wise uncle, stood in the foreground; the scaffold behind him was the picture's focus. In the deep background, like a hazy Leonardo da Vinci landscape, stood a tower in which Queen Esther stood with Ahasuerus, King of the Medes and Persians (also, in medieval legend, one the names given the Wandering Jew). Some who later saw the painting believed that the evil Haman, who plotted to destroy all the Jews, appeared as a ghostly insect swarm near the scaffold. In any case, it was clear that the symbolism of the scene vibrated in Albert's mind, though the sketches and the wash blocking-out also troubled him. He imagined this third balanced with the other two in the triptych. They became a vivid arrangement of colors communicating violence. But there was also something else.

His eyes were shut. He opened them and saw the waiting canvases, but once again felt defeat and deflation. At last he went to a chair with its back to the panels and sat. On the table beside the chair was the letter from his younger brother Artur, which he had mentioned to Konrad. Idly, he touched its envelope.

He had slipped the letter into his jacket pocket when Lisel appeared in the archway. It was late morning, but she was still in a nightgown he had bought for her. It was white, printed with violets, but she was not wearing the matching robe because of the heat. He was also now aware of the heat for the first time. He noticed she carried her head above her white shoulders as if it were indeed the fine porcelain it looked like. She stood with one hand flat on the wall, bare feet on the dark floor.

"I am disturbing you?"

"Oh, no." He gestured over his shoulder at the easels. "I am not getting much done this morning."

"I am sorry."

"It's not your fault."

"I think it must be."

"You were born a distraction of the most generous sort. Do not accept the blame the gods deserve for your beauty. Tell me now. Are you hungry for some breakfast?"

Her hand moved quickly to her stomach and rested there. She shook her head gently as if she thought something would rattle in her skull.

"I don't like to ask your housekeeper. She doesn't like me. She doesn't approve."

"Nor does she understand. She is a servant."

"She should know you are a perfect gentleman."

He smiled. "Lotte is familiar with my imperfections. I must forgive her so she will forgive my trespasses."

She frowned and again shook her head carefully.

"And you must forgive my irreverances as my good friend Father Konrad does." Albert said.

"He is a holy man," she said.

"Yes. He is." He stood. "Come now. We must see about your breakfast."

"I'm not hungry in the morning anyway. Food in the morning makes me feel sick."

He looked at her with fresh concern.

She bit her lips. She sighed. "Perhaps a little coffee then," she said.

"Good." He smiled. "And then you shall have a proper breakfast." He exited down the hall to the stairs. He called to her, "Sit down then, I'll be right back."

Descending quickly to the kitchen, he was suddenly cheered by the necessity of looking after her. As he waited in the kitchen while Lotte made up the breakfast he'd ordered, the comforting smell of coffee added to his improving mood. Then the canvas of *Hanging Haman* flashed into his mind, and the coffee he was sipping tasted bitter. He put down the cup and took from his jacket the letter from his brother, a letter he had already read many times. With every reading, the departure from his homeland became more real. He hated the letter, but he also treasured it in a special way: as a mental door through which he might escape when he needed to.

Artur was Albert's half-brother, ten years his junior, the product of a second marriage to a Jewess from Berlin. Albert's mother, a Catholic, had died when Albert was 14. Albert's father, an impulsive and cynical Jew, had made the second marriage an intense affirmation of his heritage (certainly not his faith, of which he had none), yet within one year, he returned to his broadside denunciations of all religions and traditions, including his own. At his death he was buried beside his first, Catholic, wife, as he requested in his will.

The letter was written on the creamy stationery of Artur's Manhattan emporium Entrater's:

Dear Albert,

I have hesitated a long while before writing to you for several reasons. Our last meeting upon your arrival in New York four years ago convinced me that your attitude toward me has not altered since the days of childhood. This conviction has saddened me. Indeed, it diminishes my life in ways you may not care to know, but that is not the issue here. What is of moment as I write on this grim anniversary of the shameful book-burnings is your situation and your safety. Daily, the temple of which I am a member must deal with refugees from the prison Germany is becoming. We hear terrible stories that make what little news we can read in the newspapers sound like dim echoes.

For so long I have thought of your being my older brother and your being my half-brother as the same difference: the ten years between us explained to me your disdain; my whole Jewishness compared to your half explained to me your disdain. I think I admired you for despising me! And it made perfect sense in my child's mind that a young man should argue and rebel against his father, should leave the house in a storm of manly anger, should break our hearts. And, of course, it was right and true this revolution should center on the honor of our homeland at War, and a young man who so wanted to fight for her.

I have also tried to imagine what April, 1918, was to you—fighting the Great War. I remember the day I came home from school and all the servants shushed me. You had been wounded; no one knew how badly. Then they said your right hand was gone. How could you continue as an artist without your right hand?

You came home and had to live again like a boy in our father's house. The epidemic had taken your wife and baby girl. Forgive my recalling these painful times to you. I have cause. My wife and son cannot be any less precious to me now than your Hilde and Gerta were to you.

The world seemed to be falling apart then. It was the end of the Empire. We told ourselves we could have won the Great War if we had not been betrayed. We hated so desperately (and foolishly) our 'betrayers.' Yet who were they? You were a wounded soldier grieving in your bed down the hall from my room. I could hear you groaning during the night. I heard footsteps of servants running at all hours to your room. Your suffering made me feel small and weak and afraid to become a man.

I thought you suffered as a patriot for the end of the Empire, for the loss of the King. Did you suffer over the betrayal by the 'November criminals' who signed the shameful surrender and consigned Germany to democracy instead of the gilded monarchy beloved by all?

My G-d, Albert, how our imaginations shaped the world to our desperate needs!

I work in the City, but our new house is in the country to the east. If the house we have is large enough to accommodate my mother and my wife and boy—be assured there is room enough for you. The gabled roof is slate-covered, and the landing on the second floor has an open room where the housekeeper sews, much like our house in Grünewald, which was what made this house charming to me. Our Italian cook knows more recipes for fig and other foods than suit our taste, perhaps, but her very good nature makes them more palatable.

The countryside is also pretty. There is no Spree or Havel or splendid Wannsee of hidden woods and islands and castles, but the big park in the City is graceful and we live among spacious farms.

I could go on tempting you perhaps with my pride in my new country. But I do not believe such efforts could move you. I do not forget your evaluation of my 'bourgeois goals' and our well-informed deliberations on the topics of materialism and artistic idealism. These would still sting, were I not already 'gorged on pots of honey.'

*No, we are concerned with a larger matter—with the future in Berlin and Germany, with the life of one baptized-albeit-*Mischlinge *artist whose rejection of his father's heritage would keep him from seeing that there is in politics the equivalent of what in business we bourgeois call Gresham's Law. By this is meant that bad money drives out good, and bad leadership drives out what is at least endurable. Dear Albert, it takes no astrologer or clairvoyant to read the handwriting on the German Nebuchadnezzar's wall. The message is as dire as it was for that old tyrant's son. I am a businessman, I know business:*

The financial crisis facing Germany is cataclysmic. Oh yes, Bruning did well for Germany, canceling out part of the war debt, but those debts under the Dawes & Young Plans still remain, as well as many others. And yes, Schacht's return to the Reichsbank is hopeful, but it is doubtful that any consolidated reaction will be forthcoming from the creditor countries because cooperation among economic rivals is rare in the best of times; during this depression it is inconceivable. Even Jews don't agree on the boycott of Nazi goods!

The programs which are needed to stabilize Germany from within and without cannot continue if the foreign exchange reserves in the Reichsbank continue to dwindle. I have heard rumors to this effect that make me particularly worried. Schmitt's economic policy, which would result in increased consumer spending, will only exacerbate a perilous situation. Increased consumer spending, Albert, means imports. This returns us to the critical foreign exchange problem and further, a vicious battle for raw materials between consumer producers and armament manufacturers. The Army will not stand idly by as these problems worsen.

What will be the inevitable result of this gathering storm? From this side of the Atlantic, the ranting of the Dillinger-turned-politico Hitler raises the darkest shadow of the future, the shadow of the black German eagle.

And don't expect German industrialists to raise a hand to him. No, they are paralyzed by fear of a communist solution to the economic crisis which the monarchy sired in Germany. In the end, where will this leave you, Albert—capitalist, artist, and Jew? Look about you at the others who have left and who are leaving. What are you waiting for? For the handwriting on the wall to come as a printed invitation? This then is your invitation. Mann, who is no Jew!, will be arriving in New York in so many days. I have this from friends who are meeting him. I cannot imagine what keeps you in Berlin. Maybe you think this is some tremor, not an earthquake, in the body politic. Do not delude yourself!

You may call yourself a 'German-of-Jewish-origin,' and paint them pictures out of Aryan fairytales. Or go as far as Levi did when he said if he had to conduct another Mauschel-opera, he would join the ranks of German anti-Semites.

But they would not have him, Albert, and they will not have you. The pathetic effort to define and defend Jews within German Culture will not affect where reason has no reach. It is not a shame to be a Jew, it is only a shame to be ashamed. Let me borrow an idea from your fine friend, your priest Konrad. It is our cross to bear to be a light unto the generations. But how far we must follow them into the dark to drag them out screaming has not been revealed to me. It seems to me we function far better as models than as missionaries or martyrs. You see, I am a reformed Jew, and I am arguing in favor of our flight from the dark storm in which you would only be a very little candle swiftly extinguished.

Even your Faust argues with you! 'Anxious, watching, we stand here./ When, how, where will it break forth,/ Lurking monster,/Lurking deeply with malice so great?' *You and I know the answer to that question, dear brother.*

You may not love me, I know, but that is of no consequence. Just come. Leave behind all the graves sacred to you in Germany. You cannot honor them better than with your life and your work.

With respect,
Artur Wilhelm Entrater

*

Lotte lifted the tray she had prepared for Lisel. She walked from the kitchen without disturbing Mr. Entrater's concentration. But he had finished reading the letter and folded it up. He followed the housekeeper down the long hall. How dearly he loved his brother, and how poorly he expressed it.

That night in a room across the city, Konrad and three others met to consider the final plans for the assassination of German Chancellor Hitler. It was generally agreed that simplicity, like a willingness to die in the effort, was the key to success.

CHAPTER SEVEN

ON Sunday, June 17, after Hilter's Venetian visit with his model and mentor Mussolini, a speech was given which threatened him, Hitler, directly. The speech, made in Marburg, 240 kilometers southwest of Berlin, was given by von Papen, the Vice-Chancellor of Germany.

"Things are going badly," President Hindenburg had told von Papen, whom he greatly preferred to Hitler. "See what you can do to put them right."

So out of von Papen's mouth in Marburg came the words written by Edgar Jung, von Bose, and Klausner. The first of these was well acquainted with Father Konrad Hoeffer, Albert Entrater's long-time friend.

Particular passages in the speech drew Nazi Party leader Goebbels's special attention and ire, as a red cape enraged the Spanish bull. The following was found in the Nazi's journal, copied word for word from the original text and festooned with Goebbels's feverish scholia:

> *There appears to be endless talk of a second wave which will complete the revolution. Anyone who irresponsibly toys with such ideas should not deceive himself... he who threatens the guillotine is the first to come under the knife.*

The Government is well aware of the selfishness, the lack of principal... the arrogance, which is on the rise under the guise of the German revolution.

Confidence and willingness to cooperate will not be furthered by incitement, particularly incitement of the young nor by threats against defenseless classes of the community.

The people will follow the Führer... provided every word of criticism is not immediately interpreted as malicious, provided that despairing patriots are not branded as traitors...

It is time to silence doctrinaire fanatics...

From the point of view of the "doctrinaire fanatics" like Nazi Party leader Goebbels, it was time to stop the spread of this Marburg speech. But the Vice-Chancellor had already distributed advance copies of it and had used the Catholic newspaper *Germania* as the courier of thousands of other reprints secretly disseminated through agencies that included Konrad Hoeffer.

The Marburg speech was a revelation. Let its light shine and spread, and the Nazi party would have to scurry for the holes and dark undersides of the rocks from which its members crawled. With (former General) President Hindenburg's blessing, the Army would sustain Germany, would enstate Vice-Chancellor von Papen as interim leader, and would finally restore the beloved monarchy to a more moderate right-wing ascendence. German citizens like Albert Entrater found the Marburg speech the first small flame in the darkening gloom.

And, of course, Hilter knew all this. He was doubly disgruntled to see what Mussolini had told him was so promptly coming to pass—that the Devil collects all debts, also from his minions, yea, even unto Beelzebub himself.

*

In combination with two days of excellent work at his triptych, the Marburg speech gave Albert a sudden and powerful surge of well-being, which he expressed with the decision to visit the Romanisches for the first time in many weeks. Commentary from Ludvik and others had discouraged him from returning to the fabled nightclub, but today he bought the girl a smashing green and silver evening gown at Faber's, and himself a new red tie. His heart raced like that of a soldier on his first leave. For extra company, he called Ludvik, but he was not in. He considered calling his art dealer, Maximilian, a comical quipster, but he remembered the bad experience Max had had with the brownshirts who patroled the cafes dunning contributions for the Nazi cause. Never mind the gloom, Albert shook himself free of the momentary pessimism; the brownshirts had read the Vice-Chancellor's warnings and disapprobations.

After supper, he and the girl—who had stunned even him with her breathtaking appearance—taxied north, then east up through the Kurfurstendamn bars and cafes that catered to every prediliction. He recognized the ubiquitous street performers—the jaded young men, the glittery women. (How he'd missed the energy of this most Berlin of boulevards!)

American jazz seeped from The Yellow Orchid, whose black-faced doorman was outfitted in his satin plantation attire. Nearby, the large revolving doors of the Romanisches gleamed in the yellow light. Just as he and the girl arrived, a longtime friend bolted out. Albert greeted the rushing man, but he walked past without a word. Simultaneously, two brownshirts appeared through the revolving doors. Albert's friend paced away with vigor, but the brownshirts followed and overtook him at the corner. Lisel turned away just before the man's narrow figure doubled over like a marionnette's. She put her hand on Albert's arm, though he hadn't moved. With the swiftness of experience, the brownshirts rifled the man's pockets, and just as quickly they were away down the street and into another café. When they were safely out of view, Albert went to his fallen friend and helped him to his feet. He found a taxi which drove them to an apartment that bordered on the Grünewald.

"It was my own bloody fault," his friend confessed. "Too much schnapps and von Papen's speech made me a hero."

Lisel felt the man's future and shuddered.

CHAPTER EIGHT

ON Thursday the 21st, four days following von Papen's speech at Marburg, Lisel was sitting at a restaurant with a particularly white-eyed Horst. It was a hot day again and sunny, appropriate for the summer solstice, the day the sun stands still as far north in the sky as it ever climbs. It was a poised, precipitous day. She had met Horst for lunch after a morning of tumultuous nausea.

She had little stomach for the meal, though this went unnoticed by Horst, who was mostly absorbed in testing the point of his knife against his thumb. The young corporal was patently unimpressed with von Papen's warning against a second revolutionary "wave."

"Marburg means nothing to them. Soon, they say, the Second Revolution, the real revolution, will come, the 'Night of the Long Knives.' That is what the Stormtroopers are waiting for. Some of us think they may be right. I for one take a wait-and-watch attitude." He was concluding the topic of his lunch-hour conversation. Then he put the knife down and examined the flat of his thumbnail.

"I wish you would not do that," she said at last.

He looked up, uncomprehending.

"Whenever you look at your thumb like that, you come out with something bad. I never realized that before, but now I see it is true," she said, beginning to feel that vague hollowness that made her anxious.

"I do not," he said. In a lesser man—or uniform—the tone would be called petulance.

"Yes, you do," she nearly sighed.

"Well, then it is your fault—"

"You see?"

"You do not understand, Lisel. How can you—how can I continue when you—."

A wave of nausea broke somewhere in her middle and did not stop until it reached downward to her knees, weakening them even as she sat, reaching upward to crawl at the roots of her short hair. She shivered.

"You are living with a Jew!"

Startled out of her nausea, she looked at his plate for the words he had spat out like disgusting food. She widened her eyes at him. This had an encouraging effect on the unhappy young man. He reached over and placed his palm upon her hand to steady her. At his touch, she stifled a cry. It felt as if he had burned her, and painful waves hit her from all sides. Her eyes closed and she swayed. She held onto the table with both hands. It had been two weeks—since she had moved into Mr. Entrater's apartment—since she had had a bad spell. She had hoped it would not come again, but moments before she had realized the currents were swirling over her again. It was like sliding around and around in a cool whirlpool of increasingly dark colors which soon, she knew, would become illuminated and confusing underwater scenes, like the cinema. Scenes would burst upon her inner eye, complete with insistent talk of people already engaged in conversation as if she were listening in on a telephone party line to many conversations at once.

She held onto the table at the same time. She could feel the white cloth, the thick weave of it, and at the same time she saw still blue water, a forest of pines, a hotel surrounded by soldiers in black uniforms. She could see simultaneously inside another building's interior, a stairway with a shining wooden bannister and dark wooden walls; there were women wearing white blouses and black ties and black skirts running up and down a wide staircase. She could hear the noise of their heels clicking on the stone stairs, and in the distance, she could hear the sound of typewriters. She saw a hotel where men were lying with boys, and outside it, a circular driveway spat gravel up at speeding black cars. She saw and heard revolvers slipping out of brown leather holsters…

"Lisel!" Horst said.

She opened her eyes. Above Horst's head was a mirror that reflected the restaurant. On the dark wooden walls were portraits of patrons that contrasted painfully with the brightness of the street outside. Sunlight was glancing off a car window. As a memory rather than a vision, she saw what she had seen days earlier, the Sunday night of the von Papen speech when Mr. Entrater's friends had gathered together and eaten a great deal of food. She had felt cold then, too, and was falling asleep on the couch in the midst of them like a child; someone had put a sweater over her. The remembered image was horrible, like facing a giant snail eye to eye, its pug Pekinese nose pressed up against her face, but its skin, oh horrible! slippery and pink, with the smell of salt water and blood…

"Horst, she said, blinking.

"You're still sick."

It was her turn to be petulant. "It's not my fault. I want to go home." Now she understood what she had seen that night when her own sweater had started the waves. She had escaped that night into sleep.

He did not move. After he carefully arranged his fork and knife on the plate, he put both his palms flat on the white tablecloth. He looked at his thumb, then shook his head at the gesture.

"This has got to stop," he ordered.

She tried to smile. "I'm not enjoying it."

"You should join the League of German Girls. You should be a model carrier of the National Socialist world-view. You should dedicate yourself to the group, to service, and physical fitness for motherhood."

She moved her head back on her slim neck, felt her shoulder muscles hold her up more firmly.

"Or—" he said breathlessly.

She tilted her head. Her now-short blonde hair curved just under her cheek, and the mirror above Horst caught and reflected its midday light. "Or?" she repeated.

She could feel what it cost him to say the next words and knew them before she heard:

"Or it is all over between us," he said.

She couldn't help it: a smile blossomed like a flower. She covered her mouth.

"You do not understand how serious this is," he said. "It is not only filthy and disgusting, what you are doing, but it is dangerous."

"I am not doing anything filthy and disgusting. I know what filthy and disgusting is—" he lowered his eyes—"as you very well know, and I am not a party to it. That is another Party of which I am not a member."

"Lisel, keep your voice down and do not say such things. You must not say—" he was terribly upset. "How can I—I?—endanger the future of this society by consorting with such a woman? What cruelty that Kriemhild Woman is ever the downfall of what is best in Man!"

She stood. "Listen to me, you Horst Dörner. I knew you before ever you went off to university and put on that uniform and when you came around making moony eyes at me like any other boy in Buttelstädt. We come into this world naked and out naked we shall also go. As for 'future society,' it is *entirely* safe if what you call consorting between us is what is worrying you. You conceited—" she couldn't think of the word; it was a picture of a bird that Father Konrad had showed her that puffed itself up to attract during "courtship" and the word *courtship* in Father's voice kept getting in the way of—"*blowfish*!"

At surrounding tables people were careful not to observe this scene of the rifle-backed Liebstandarte officer being humiliated by the young woman. There was something primal about the confrontation: Beauty (Lisel) standing up to the Beast (politics). The waiter who had been approaching the table to clear away the dishes stopped short and gestured with his hands, both slowing himself down and offering palms-up contrition to avoid interrupting the encounter.

As if she had said nothing at all, Horst looked up at her and said, menacingly, "Where do you think you are *going*?"

She folded her bare arms across the breast of her blue blouse. "Why? Do you intend to arrest me?"

"I could."

"How you talk."

"I could," he repeated.

"I'm going back to the only person who doesn't make me see terrible things," she said.

"The Jew."

"He is kind."

"I've been a fool," he said, also standing abruptly, leaving money on the table and walking roughly past Lisel, murmuring by habit as a final farewell, "Heil Hitler!"

Meanwhile, Horst's hero, the German Chancellor, was being similarly rebuffed by the German Defense Minister, General von Blomberg. The Marburg speech had reached President Hindenburg at his estate in the north at Neudeck, and Hitler had flown there on the wings of his plane *Immelman* to see whether rumors of Hindenburg's displeasure would indeed result in martial law under the Nazi-despising elite German Army Corps. Blomberg's curt treatment of Hitler, as he barred the way to the President, who was the only real order principle left in Germany, was also in the form of the ultimatum Mussolini had so prophetically predicted: Hitler could choose legitimate power—or the bastard, Röhm.

CHAPTER NINE

THAT night, Lisel declined an invitation to the theater with Mr. Entrater and some friends, and after a cold supper with Lotte in the kitchen, she visited the bookcases that filled the long wall of the study. The medical encyclopedia was her need, which she found, then the desired volume. She read under a yellow light with uncharacteristic concentration. A particular passage caught her attention and she read it several times.

She slipped her hand into her blouse. Her breasts were firm, but not tender. Neither were her nipples, which her touching made hard. She rose and approached a framed mirror over a side table. After moving the table lamp to one side, she unbuttoned her blouse and took each breast from the brassiere. Her heart pounded. The usually pale nipples were suffused with a dusky color. She moved closer to the mirror, rearranged the lamp and shade, but the images remained unaltered. She placed a hand over her belly. Her eyes burned.

"What are you doing?" came Lotte's harsh voice from behind.

"Nothing," she said, covering herself.

"I cleaned this room today."

"Yes."

She put away the book and went to her room under Lotte's watch. Her brain was swarming. Sleep never came that night. Her young mind was under siege from all sides. Shame, rage, and fear swept through her, alone and in combination. Father Konrad, the three brownshirts—each of these also appeared from the deepest well in her subconscious.

The next day, in league with fate, she met with Father Konrad, who had come for a visit. She sat on a couch downstairs in the living room, and he sat beside her, his own worried hands folded in his lap. Like the girl, he was also suffering internal sea changes. As he looked at her, it was hard for him to remember how she had dressed when she'd first returned from the country. Now with her hair cut short and styled and the fine fashionable beige suit Albert had gotten her, she looked like a member of a different class.

For Lisel's part, everything about this late Friday afternoon continued to feel otherworldly. The big white living room didn't look like a room people would live in. Its high white walls with huge paint-splashed canvases looked like some futuristic lobby. The windows had no hanging draperies, and the few pieces of large furniture looked like boulders or rain-sodden clouds.

"Well," Father Konrad said.

She looked over into the face of the priest. It was long and reminded her of a hound's. He had had his hair cut; it used to look like long ears. It was hard for her to look at him.

"You want to speak to me?"

"I didn't say so, but..."

He smiled. "What is it, then?"

"You didn't really want the newspaper."

His smile vanished. "I wanted it, yes."

She had been aware for some time of his intention to murder the German Chancellor.

"What is it, then?" he repeated gently.

"I—would like to know, Father, which is the worse sin?"

"The worst?" he nodded, hiding behind a grammatical correction, while the question loomed over him like an Everest.

"Yes," she said.

He spoke quietly. "Perhaps taking the life of another."

"To take the life of *any* other?" She waited solemnly, like a schoolgirl.

"No. Not perhaps of any other."

"To take the life of evil?"

He shook his head. "If one knew of the evil—"

"Father, to fail to take such a life would be a sin, would it not?"

"If one were certain of the evil, then perhaps it would. You see, our Lord tells us that to *think* a crime is equal to commiting it, so the gradation among sins is a man-made concept and illusion. Moreover, *certain* knowledge of evil is as rare as certain knowledge of good."

"But God is good, Father. I am certain of that."

"Yes."

"And there is evil I am certain of as well. You have considered this question, Father."

"Yes," he said. "It is an integral part of my business, so to speak." He smiled.

"It is more to you than that, Father."

He hesitated. Again his smile vanished.

"It is important to me, because the brownshirts, when they raped me, made me pregnant." Lisel paused.

"Pregnant?"

"Yes."

"I see."

"There is evil in me now."

"Not necessarily. There was evil done, but good may come from evil. Moral questions—"

"It may. But it does not."

"You are certain."

"Yes, Father. I am certain. As you are certain."

His throat tightened to a tourniquet. "I only wish I could answer your question more satisfactorily. It is a Jesuit's holiday. Unfortunately, I am no Jesuit."

"How do you see me, Father?"

Konrad spoke slowly. "I see you as a child of God. And as the victim of a terrible crime."

"And what shall I do with myself now?"

"I cannot answer that simply. Certain alternatives are unacceptable under any circumstances."

"You see, it is the action *and* the thought that ruins me."

"Dear Lisel, you are not ruined, not in God's eyes."

"Father—"

"You are a lovely young woman still, and in due time—"

"No, Father! I am not that anymore." She paused. "What would you do, Father, if you were me?"

"I would not abort the child." He broke off. Behind his eyes the ache had risen again, the ache that had become his constant companion. Through the large open window, the air carried the scent of coming rain. He rose and went to it, stood by the window, and looked out. All the while, her stare was transfixing him. Konrad shook his head slowly.

"It's so hot this June," he attempted. "No wonder all we talk of is murder." He turned to her. "Murder is in the air."

"Father," she said then, barely above a whisper.

He returned to the couch and sat beside her. "Yes?"

"I know you are planning to kill the Chancellor."

He half exhaled and forced a smile. "Really now."

"I have seen it."

"And how have you seen it?"

"Through your own eyes when you've touched me, to help me rise, to move through a door. First, I have seen a gunsite, yes? Aimed from wooden benches at a parade. I heard the names: *Immelman* for one; *America*—which is the name of a train. Yes? And then there have been explosions to be blamed on airplanes, but this is only a story so he will not become a martyr. It is important that he is not martyred. Last," she said slowly, "I see a shape like this." She cupped her hands together. "Like a bottle of," she pronounced the word with particular sophistication, "*Cointreau*. But you call it a *clam*—it is an explosive." She waited.

"You have heard idle conversations, Lisel, or rumors."

"I have heard you, Father, in your mind."

His eyes narrowed to slits.

"Listen to me," she continued, now warning. "You are worried for a man named Erich, yes?—Erich Weiss?"

"No," he lied. "I know of no one by that name."

"He is good with explosives but given to personal explosions of his own; he admires too greatly a man named Bakunin." She pronounced the Russian anarchist's name as if she had heard it. "He is a risk to you, Father. A grave risk."

The priest reached out a hand to her, barely listening.

"He is too wild." Suddenly her eyes were wide. "Father, what is it?"

"Lisel," he said too gently.

"Father, I have told no one. I swear it. And I will tell no one."

"No, of course not." Then his hand touched hers.

"No," she whispered. "Please—"

She recoiled from his touch and stood. Konrad moved toward her again, but she walked away from him so that he watched the curve of her back. By the window, her knees began to buckle, her face paled, and she turned as if to ward him off with a raised hand. His small eyes were like diamonds.

All at once she looked straight into his eyes. "Father," she said in warning. Now she was no longer looking *at* him, but through him, to a distant corner of the room.

"What is it? Tell me," he repeated, as one might to break a spell. "Tell me, Lisel."

He was caught up in the girl's focus. And then as if having received an answer, he turned in the direction of her unwavering line of sight. At the same moment the sun, moving from behind a cloud, flashed through the largest window, and at the edge of the priest's view a shadow flickered. Inarticulately, the girl called out a word or phrase. The priest blinked, listening. Again, he blinked, when a blinding flash of light came at him from the hallway mirror that knocked him sideways, and down he fell, striking his face on the curved arm of a chair. A sharp pain exploded in his neck.

For a moment, the pain stunned him. Then when he had opened and refocused his eyes, he could only see a newspaper headlined *Elsholtz Murdered!* tossed on the floor. He shook his head, cleared it; then to his rear he heard a familiar voice. He lifted himself and turned. Albert's dark face floated into view, across the room by the windows, where he had rushed and was kneeling beside the pale-faced girl who lay collapsed and unconscious by the couch. Konrad's eyes burned. His friend was cradling the girl's face.

"Albert."

"What happened?"

The priest swallowed. "I'm not certain. She had a seizure. It was *you* just now?"

"She's barely breathing."

"Yes," the priest said, trying to calm himself—the exploding light had been the sun flashing off the mirror. It was Albert who had knocked him down, rushing to the girl. But then—what had the girl *seen*?

"We were only talking," Konrad said.

"About what!" Albert asked sharply.

"How is she? Is she all right?"

"Was it one of your bloody interrogations?"

"No. Of course not." Konrad had gotten to his feet and was rubbing at the ache in his neck. "Is she breathing?"

"Yes, she's breathing."

"You gave me quite a jolt." His head was spinning.

"I'm sorry," Albert said. "I was distracted."

"You saw her collapse?" Konrad asked.

"Just the last of it," Albert said.

Lisel moaned then; her eyes began to flutter under the lids. She murmured as in sleep.

"What does she say?"

Albert shook his head. "I cannot tell."

"She seems more peaceful," Konrad said.

Indeed, her breathing had quieted. Albert pressed his ear to her heart, listened, felt her cheek with his own. Her face was regaining color, and she had warmed noticeably. He decided to lift her, but his impairment and Lisel's position by the couch made this difficult. Konrad went to him, knelt down to help, forcing his two good arms under her legs and back. Albert continued to support her head. Her breathing now was slow and calm. Konrad rose, the girl and he forming a kind of cross. Albert hovered by like a watchful shadow.

"To her room?"

Albert nodded.

Because she was tall, Albert was needed to help with her up the stairs. Down the hall to one of the guest rooms, they rested. For the last several steps, their hands formed a trinity joined in the task. When Albert was not examining Lisel's face, he was searching into Konrad's eyes. Finally, her lips parted in a gusty breath as her head found the hollow of the soft pillow.

Albert sat down on one of the two needlepoint chairs beside the bed and motioned Konrad to sit likewise, but he remained standing.

"What happened?" Albert asked again, more calmly.

"I'm not sure."

"She had a vision?"

"I don't know. Perhaps. Listen to me, Albert. Listen carefully. Take her away while you can get your money. To England if not America. Someplace surrounded by a vast moat of water."

"Why?"

"Because she is in danger."

"From her Nazi boyfriend? I don't think so."

"She is living with a Jew."

"Is that what you were talking about with her?"

"Yes."

"Kon?"

"Believe me, damn it, will you!" Konrad stopped.

It was then, of course, in the sudden silence, that Albert could hear it, the unmistakable tone of confession just below the surface of the worry for Lisel. And when he looked again at the girl, he nearly saw the truth whole. Characteristically, he sought to disengage himself from it, for like so many, Albert found certain truths corrosive, particularly those that threatened his fundamental trusts and assumptions. A malevolence bound Konrad to Lisel; that, Albert sensed palpably. Indeed, a separate malevolence had grown up about his old friend. For his own peace of mind, however, Albert would disregard this; he would go on dealing with the "new" Konrad as if he were the old. Albert had suffered enough losses in his life.

"You look tired," he told Konrad.

"Yes."

"Frazzled." He tried to smile. "And you were right, of course, quite right as usual: the paper is screaming with the news of Elsholtz. Filled with every gory detail." Albert referred to the headline story of the bloody mutilation of an estate caretaker, a Nazi, whose murder had stirred cries of outrage and revenge. "The Nazis are blaming Meissner, who is close to Catholic circles. No surprise in that."

"No." Konrad understood the rules of the game now, his old friend's limited capacity for emotional or spiritual support.

"Still for the Nazis, Catholics aren't as bad as the Jews." Albert said.

"No."

"Although, as you've said, Hitler knows, even if the Pope does not, that Christ was a Jew. Are you all right?"

"Yes." Konrad said. "Yes, I am fine."

"I think I shall get you an aspirin."

"All right."

"Sit, have a bit of rest."

Konrad managed a smile. "I've a devil of a headache."

"This bloody weather doesn't help."

"No."

Albert left.

The air in the room was soft and still. The priest settled into another chair across from Albert's. The room, he noticed, had changed since the girl's arrival: the flowered bud vase on the night table held a strongly scented tea rose; there was a lace doily over the dresser; opaque glass jars of powders and perfumes crowded the dresser top. Within reach lay a shining silver comb, brush, and mirror. He massaged his neck. Albert returned with water and aspirin tablets which Konrad downed in a swallow.

"Gave me quite a jolt, bashing by me like that," Konrad said.

Albert resumed his seat.

"So how do you see all this then?" Konrad continued.

"Elsholtz, you mean?"

"Well, yes, of course."

"Well." Albert smiled. "Of course, I see Durer's *Knight, Death, and the Devil*—because I even *think* in triptychs these days."

"But I think there will be punishment for the Elsholtz murder."

"Yes, most certainly."

"Great punishment."

"Are you in danger, then?"

Konrad nodded. "I think perhaps I am."

"I see."

"I am indirectly connected. You will also be in danger, Albert, particularly —"

"Kon," Albert interrupted. "Your God came to Earth to recreate the world in a divine image, and I have always loved Him and *you* for it—"

"Not to *recreate*, old friend. *Redeem*. You always

emphasize the artistic image over the divine act, as if God uses a paintbrush instead of a sword."

"A sword? The Cross? Forgive me, I cannot argue with you. You always beat me. I see only an abused child here, and you—"

"The complications of life in the face of moral simplicity. Ever the problem—yes?"

Albert shook his head in defeat. Konrad regarded him intently.

"*Agape* and *phonos*—this is the true question. How can the first become the second?"

"I don't know Greek."

"Greek to us both!" The priest's eyes were bright stones.

"Please—"

"Don't worry. You'll be spared the answer."

The girl stirred, sighed, and turned over. Albert stood and unrolled the light blanket by her feet, laying it gently over her, although the room was warm with the June breeze through the window.

"Poor Egg," he whispered.

Konrad watched. His confusion turned to an aching guilt over the girl. "I liked that story," he said, an intentionally idle response to "Egg"—a character in an Agatha Christie mystery that Albert had given him.

"Oh, yes," Albert said, resuming his seat. "Ludvik gave me the book. Always charming, Frau Christie."

"I have returned the book, yes?"

"Oh, yes, I'm sure."

"I returned a book to Ludvik that I never borrowed!"

"I know the experience." Albert nodded.

Konrad glanced at the girl. "Has she told you of her new condition?"

"Well, of course, she says very little, but her mind develops on a daily basis, quite extraordinarily. On the physical side, there are no apparent abnormalities; there are no complaints she makes."

"No cause for concern, as you see it."

"And you?"

Konrad walked close to Lisel and rested his hand on her forehead.

"Has she spoken to *you* about anything?" Albert asked worriedly.

"Oh no, she has said nothing. Gellman has seen her?"

"Gellman and Stern. They call it a nervous breakdown precipitated by the attack. What can they say? But she is certainly not mentally ill. In fact, as I suggested, she has improved on the whole, even her intelligence."

"She is cool now."

"Yes, that's been the pattern."

"She has the face of an angel."

"Yes." Albert paused. "The seizure only happens when stimulation—"

"I know."

Albert stood. "If you'll stay with her, I'll run downstairs for the paper."

"Thank you," said the priest. "I promise you, she will be safe."

Konrad rose to stand by the girl for a moment after

Albert had left. Then he walked to the open window. The aspirin had taken the edge off his pain, but like any palliative, it could not reach down to the root of the problem. For the briefest instant, he admitted to himself, when she had first revealed her knowledge of him and in doing so had made herself a threat, for that briefest instant he had wished her dead. He shook his head at this recognition—another first, another first experience in a life that had been so carefully purposeful and, so he had always thought, so carefully under control.

Who are we when a stranger appears in the mirror and when the thoughts that had lulled us to sleep no longer come to mind? In the privacy of his turmoil, he heard many internal voices. He tried to achieve a lost serenity by listening to each, one by one. But pushing through the friendly murmurings, the large and small syllogisms that had formed the net of his thoughts and actions, shouted the proclamation of Hitler—*The Theologian*, they called him—and in the shouting silenced Konrad's Word: "*Patriotism transmutes individual unselfishness into national egoism! This unqualified devotion is the very basis of the freedom to use power without moral constraint! Thus the unselfishness of individuals makes for the selfishness of nations.*"

It was the perfect parody of Christian ethics, of so much he had held dear. Of himself.

Then, irresistibly, Konrad's own still, small voice answered, "Thus *agape* becomes *phonos.* Thus, in the end, the moral priest becomes the murderer!"

He heard the voice of a singing child he had heard in the street: "*No evil priest can prevent us from/ Feeling we are the children of Hitler/ We follow not Christ but Horst Wessel/ Away with the incense and holy water/ The Church can go hang for all we care!"*

Then Lisel's dark eyes darted under the lids and she made several small cries. Startled, Konrad went to her and placed his hand on her forehead as Albert entered the room. She opened her eyes, saw Mr. Entrater, smiled, then looked up at Father Konrad and felt his palm. An image of bone and blood smashed against her skull with the weight of his hand—Lisel threw up both her hands to push him away.

"What is it? What did you see?" Albert cried. All the fear of Buttelstädt was in his voice.

She and the priest exchanged a look. But Konrad quickly relaxed in exhaustion. His anxiety had been at such a high pitch that he could hardly sustain it and certainly not raise it. He leaned against the dresser with the silver brushes. Lisel, in the space of relief, saw again the image that had awakened her. She began to cry, helplessly, like a child. "Father, oh Father—"

Albert put the newspaper into Konrad's hands. He sat down on the bed beside Lisel, patted her arm, and spoke soothingly to her.

Standing by the bureau, Konrad read the news article about the Elsholtz murder. Albert looked in his direction. He noticed the characteristic pressing together of Konrad's lips as he read, and the narrow focus of the eyes, which were always, it seemed, one pair of glasses in arrears.

CHAPTER TEN

THREE days later on Monday, June 25th, the SS at Gestapo headquarters at 8 Prinz Albrechstrasse in Berlin filed the following report from Colonel Frederich Kostler regarding the arrests of Rudolf Goetz, Josef Braun, Erich Weiss, and Konrad Hoeffer:

At one p.m. on June 23 outside the post office building in Essen, pursuant to a call from Philip Greiss, pastry chef for the Karl Ernst wedding party, Rudolf Goetz and Josef Braun were arrested, having falsely presented themselves as temporary busboy and waiter respectively for the Ernst wedding, which the Führer would be attending this Thursday (6/28).

Details reveal an assassination attempt on the Führer's life involving a high explosive in the form of a small bottle, such as one for Cointreau … Goetz has implicated Erich Weiss, a known anarchist and maker of the explosive, and Konrad Hoeffer, a Catholic priest targeted for some time by us as a potential enemy of the Reich (as in connection with … Meissner and the recent Elsholtz murder). Thus far, he has said nothing more.

On Saturday the 24th, Weiss and Hoeffer were arrested at two p.m. in the Anhalter Station in Berlin, holding third-class tickets for Essen. Hoeffer, in priest's attire, carried no luggage. But Weiss's suitcase contained uniforms for domestic service and a quantity of cyclomite, a known explosive ...

At this time, it appears the scheme involved only these four ... Braun, who was 62, was found dead of a coronary infarction in his cell on the morning of the 24th. Weiss and Hoeffer have so far admitted nothing...

Leads in connection to each of the four are being sought. In this regard, we believe the technique of the "Long Rope" should be employed, as all members of the Essen wedding have been reviewed for the Führer's safety, and in light of the Marburg atmosphere, we should proceed with efficiency and tact ... The Catholics particularly may make a show about Hoeffer, one of theirs, although the Elsholtz murder may have served to sufficiently stifle their zeal, if only on a temporary basis...

Dr. M—has been brought in to "examine" Father Hoeffer, who has taken a "vow of silence" for unholy reasons ...

Weiss is a more promising prospect as he shows a special fear of fire.

F. Kostler
6-25-34

*

As we know, Karl Ernst, a key Stormtroop leader from Berlin, was married in the town of Essen on June 28, with German Chancellor Hitler in attendance. But the "Long Rope" technique, according to which Kostler's suspects were given extraordinary opportunities to betray themselves, and others, proved an overly cautious approach, particularly in regard to Albert Entrater, who came under suspicion thirty-six hours later. We know his role in the Hitler assassination was minimal at best, but we also know the connection of Konrad Hoeffer and Lisel Ganz in his apartment was not. Further, we may assume, though no hard evidence exists to confirm this, that Leibstandarte Corporal Horst Dörner, the model's obsessive admirer, intervened at some distant level on the girl's behalf and disguised even further the threat she presented to the future of the Nazi Reich.

CHAPTER ELEVEN

TWO days following Konrad's disappearance, they watched the sunset in a silence of mourning. Albert, Ludvik, and Lisel were in the studio. The warm June night made the smell of oil paint especially strong; the even heavier, slightly gagging odor of linseed oil also hung in the air. They let the dark enter the room without turning on a light.

The sunset had been one to command such a response. The delicacies of pastels, pink-lavender-yellow, had burst on the horizon hidden by the buildings of Berlin until the colors spilled orange-almost-to-red. This last was a color that drew the eye in, that laughed at human weakness which so desires what utterly consumes it. The sunset's final signature was a lurid purple, followed by the moonless black of familiar uniforms, decorated with medals and stars.

Ludvik spoke first in the dark of departed friends: "Whose food are our lions eating now?" he asked, approaching the table laden with dinner by Lotte, who noticed that the Czech journalist was trembling.

Ludvik turned on a light. Lisel blinked. She looked at the men, seeking out Mr. Entrater's calm face. He looked like he was in pain. She wondered if his stomach hurt him again. Ludvik reached into his faded jacket pocket for the reporter's notebook he had been forbidden to use officially since the previous October. Still, there it was, up to date, filled with information.

"Racosczy has returned to the land of his forebears," Ludvik read from his notes.

"Palestine?" Albert said.

"Please," Ludvik said. "Hungary. Budapest."

"You need to examine your notebook for that information?" Albert teased, knowing it to be true. Ludvik was fastidious in all things, checking even himself as a source more than twice.

"He finally became embarrassed to accept your hospitality," Ludvik said, seating himself carefully with food. "Thank God, I am beyond shame, to paraphrase someone-or-other." He plunged a forkful of parslied potatoes into his mouth and hummed to himself over their flavor.

"He had abandoned my hospitality, as you call it," Albert said, "for quite some time. I don't think I've seen him since late May."

"I think actually it was his actress he was ashamed to sponge off anymore," said Ludvik. "She's an Aryan and still allowed to act. She makes better and better money as the Jewesses have left the boards."

"Did he love her?" Albert asked.

Ludvik swallowed, then answered sarcastically, "Can there be love between a Jew and an Aryan?"

"I thought he loved her," Albert said.

"I also heard that Edgar Jung was quietly picked up last night," Ludvik said.

"Edgar Jung?"

"One of Konrad's acquaintances," the journalist explained. It was the first mention of their absent friend's name that night. "It was Jung that drafted most of the Marburg speech."

"Ah," Albert breathed. "He signed his own death warrant then."

Ludvik turned to Albert who was standing by the table of bottles. "And have you perhaps discovered anything today?"

"Nothing," Albert cut him off. "I'm afraid that while I can feed a few friends, I can't manage to save the world."

"I didn't mean Jung."

"Yes, I know." Albert clenched his right hand into a fist—only there was no hand, no fist, just the phantom pain. Because he wore no jacket that warm night, the others could see the tensing in the forearm muscles. It was quiet in the studio. Lisel stood up and went to him. She said nothing, just formed a kind of pair with him, against attack.

"In point of fact, I sent lawyers—*Aryan* lawyers—to No. 8 Prinz Albrechtstrasse, into their stinking bowels after they took Konrad away. People disappear down that hole." He poured himself a large glass of wine. "I even sent Lotte this morning. Now the poor old thing comes back to me with her name on the list, and she tells me," his voice broke, he covered it with a cough, "no good German woman should serve a Jew." He drank down half the wine. "And that is what I discovered today."

"Did you ever consider going *yourself*?" Ludvik said gently.

"Going myself?"

"Yes."

"Going myself, how?"

"To see certain of your friends."

"Oh. Certain of my friends, how? Who? No, dear Ludvik, there are no *certain* of my friends."

"I see."

"No doubt you do."

Albert finished off a glass of wine and poured himself another.

"Apparently they arrested twelve," Ludvik said, examining his notebook intently. "Nine from Deutsche Jungenschaft."

"Oh yes? Well, that's what the bastards say in their godforsaken rag of a newspaper. My God!" Albert laughed. "Have all the bloody assassins of Europe gone to sleep? Or just become Nazis?"

"It would take a purge now, to make a real difference," Ludvik said. "A succession of perfectly timed assassinations with front-page shock. The likelihood of such events is slim. But I have long believed that what men can imagine, men can do."

"Do what?" Albert said, turning.

"Whatever I can."

"Well, that is what we all do, is it not?"

"No, not all."

Albert shook his head. "Your self-confidence is truly a gift."

"Sadly, it is not an inspiration." Ludvik paused. "You think because you live in a big house, because your mother was a *shiksa*, that you are above all this—yes? If that is what you think, you are a shadow of a man!"

Lisel laid her hand on Ludvik's arm.

He turned on her. "All right then, Witch, what do you see now?"

"A friend saying more than he should," Lisel said.

"This *friend* is a bloody fake!" he looked at Lisel. "Go on, you damn witch, tell me what you see."

She spoke gently. "I only see your books in the great library where Mr. Entrater took me Saturday."

"Which books?" Ludvik said with derision.

"All of them, of course," she said.

"That is absurd."

She smiled. "You will write many."

"Masterworks," Albert encouraged.

Ludvik's mood improved. "Yes, but in whose opinion?" he laughed. He continued in a humorous vein. "What a shame, eh, Albert? Here Lisel is an Aryan, able to earn a living, and she has the one profession anathema to Nazis. They're afraid of fortune-tellers although they keep astrologers in secret!"

"They're afraid of everything," said Albert. "That's why they're bullies."

"Revisionist bullies," said Ludvik. "They rewrite the *Manifesto* by replacing *Jew* wherever you read *bourgeois*."

"Then there is the religious view, which Konrad would say if he were here," Albert spoke soberly. "When one incarnates a new god, one also incarnates a new devil. 'And our new German god builds his church on the Rock of Röhm, and the Devil must wear a Jewish face,'" he completed Konrad's favorite speech with the priest's special sense of timing and emphasis.

"I think we shall miss that man," Ludvik said.

"Yes."

"Very much." Ludvik swallowed. "I spoke out of turn before, Albert. I'm sorry."

"We are both sorry."

They listened to the street sounds of cars. In the parks, fireflies joined in phosphorescent copulations. Ludvik rose. Albert accompanied him to the stairs.

"I am thinking of leaving, too," Ludvik said. "Going back home to Prague."

"You can stay here," Albert said.

"I am no longer at ease in Berlin. It is not the city I knew. If and when I have the trainfare," he added with a smile.

"Well. I am unique among us, then. I have nowhere to go," Albert said. "I was born here."

"You don't have to die here," Ludvik said.

"I don't believe it will come to that."

"Even after last year at Marienbad when they murdered Lessing?" Ludvik pressed.

"But there is also the Marburg speech," Albert said. "And the Army will not stand by and allow the country to be debauched."

"This is not the Army you fought with in '18," Ludvik said.

"Nevertheless. Albert shook his head. "Hitler may be neurotic, but he is not mad. He wants to rule Germany, and is smart enough to know that Germany cannot be raped, she must be seduced."

Lisel flinched perceptibly.

"One way or another, she winds up in bed with the Devil," said Ludvik, "pregnant with Nazi bastards. This is no storm that will blow away."

"Your views are no less matters of faith than my own."

"Wishful thinking is not faith."

"Then I will be Pangloss," Albert said, "and shall deserve my fate."

There was a brief apologetic silence. It was understood that the argument was moot.

"I dearly hope I am wrong," Ludvik said. He nodded to Lisel and shook Albert's hand.

"If you decide to remain, call."

"Yes, of course." Ludvik smiled sadly. "There is no one else."

Lisel put her hand lightly on Ludvik's arm. "Not to Prague," she said, "go to Lisbon."

Terrified, Ludvik took the stairs.

"He will not be back," Lisel said.

"Perhaps."

"No."

"I am sorry, then."

He went to the phonograph and started a record. He listened to it for a few moments, then turned to her.

"It's a nice tune," he said, pouring himself more wine.

"Yes."

"It's American." He nodded, as if he'd said something of meaning. He looked up. "It was a month ago yesterday that I sat—stood—like this with Konrad, here… that's a question: 'One little month'—who said that?"

She shook her head. Albert was making an effort to swallow; he looked nauseated.

"You musn't drink anymore."

"'*One little month*,'" he said. "That was Hamlet. We have Faust. And Luther. Konrad told me about Luther." He paused. "Konrad liked to argue with me. Always won. Fairly. Didn't have to let him, like the others." He noticed her lavender dress and her white shoulders. "Do you know what Faust wanted?" he said. "One moment he wished would never end. One moment like that. Have you ever lived in a moment you wished would never end?"

"I don't know," she said. "Does one know?"

He opened his eyes wide to focus on her. "You say the most remarkable things now. Are you the same silly girl I once painted?"

"Was I so silly then?"

He nodded sincerely. "Yes."

"Well, perhaps you have grown sillier from drink, and by comparison I seem wiser."

He laughed. "Wonderful! Yes, undoubtedly!" he said. "Tell me: does the smallest tree in the Grünewald have deeper roots in Germany than I? The Jews have been here for 700 years!"

"I cannot answer."

"No, of course you cannot."

He watched her from accross the yellow light of electric lamps flickering in the night. He knew just how to stroke that on with a brush.

"I must tell you," Albert said.

"Yes?"

"I could not go for him myself. Konrad. I could not." His voice broke. He half-whispered, "It was too bloody *dangerous*."

"Yes."

The needle caught, and the record skipped round and round. The needle complained rhythmically of the meaningless journey, like a planet about the sun. She went to him, and he saw Konrad's sad face. Tears rolled down his cheeks, and he heard a small child sobbing. Outside, a cloud covered the moon. He laid his head on her narrow shoulder and her arms circled around him. Inside, she felt the cells of new life taking their form with a relentless precision. To the rhythmic click of the broken record, he wept in his mother's arms for the loss of his brother.

CHAPTER TWELVE

CONSIDER the following from Kiyoshi: *Art is the shadow of the bird.*

The implications buried in this simple idea are fascinating and numerous. The bird is life, the passing scene, or if you will, history itself. Under certain circumstances, the shadow is bird-like, representational. Under different circumstances, it is an abstraction, a plane geometric projection very different from its source. The artist in this allegory is the sun, whose position in the sky above the bird determines the shape that the shadow will take.

But how do we explain a shadow when there is *no* bird?

It is this question which was so astonishingly illustrated in the 1933 allegorical drama *The Mensuren* ("The Duel") that an account of the play and its author follows here (The notes of journalist Ludvik Brezina, who reviewed the play in its single performance in 1933, serve as the primary source):

> *It is commonly known that the play's author raised money for production by selling the furnishings of a house he was renting. When later challenged in a Munich court, he insisted that as an artist he was "not subject to human laws and standards." In retrospect, his pronouncement vibrates with meaning.*

As The Mensuren begins, a generalized map appears on stage in the form of a giant spiderweb. A large and hairy black spider sleeps in the web, downstage-left, aware nonetheless that on the branch of a great tree sits an old bird, which has the power to smash the web and eat him. (After some initial puzzlement, Brezina interprets the spider as Chancellor Hitler and the old bird as German President Hindenburg.)

The appearance on the stage, downstage-right, of a flying beetle, a firefly (Stormtroop leader Ernst Röhm, Brezina decides), *suddenly rouses the spider from its sleep to the silent acknowledgement that this web is big enough only for one bug, himself. The spider extends one of its black legs, and Beetle Röhm retreats in mid-air above the stage. The wires break and sway, threatening to swing the beetle right into the web.*

In retreat, the beetle flies backward away from the web, nearly over the audience, causing a general outcry of mingled fear and excitement. (As Brezina points out months later, "This was undoubtedly Röhm's agreement to put the Stormtroopers on leave for the month of July, 1934!") *The old bird on the branch ruffles its regal feathers in disdainful acceptance. The spider whispers almost inaudibly in its sleep, "My breath will last longer than the old bird's—meaning, it is surmised, Hindenburg's.*

In a later scene, the web is played by three look-alikes. They are costumed in white sticky material and joined together by loose, sticky ropes. Finely choreographed, they move as one against the black backdrop. A fierce little grey man now appears in uniform, a black spider embroidered on each sleeve, obsessively jerking a decorated yo-yo. ("It's Hitler, of course," Brezina writes. Metamorphized!") *The web-trinity mumbles invectives to the little man about the Beetle, who is now hibernating at a pond to the south.*

Suddenly, the stage is filled with astrologer-magicians in black robes patterned with moon and stars, with tall black cone-peaked, star-studded hats. As the little man rushes off-stage doing elaborate tricks with his yo-yo, he is replaced by another character who is taken by Brezina to represent General von Reichenau of the German Army. Dressed as an exterminator, von Reichenau despises insects, especially beetles. When the trinity whisper lies about Beetle Röhm in his ear, he passionately turns and cries, "The Beetles are arming themselves silently." His words also deal with the single-mindedness of the Coleoptera order, of which the firefly is a specie.

The little man returns, stage-right, snapping his yo-yo right up into his hand, inclining his head to the audience for applause for his magical control. The exterminator stamps a high-booted leg. Spiderman makes a palms-up, what's-it-all-about? gesture. The exterminator yells, "Now is the time to act!"

"Don't say more than what has to be said," Spiderman says. The cryptic words somehow soothe the excited exterminator, and Spiderman puts his arm around the exterminator's shoulder, who eyes the embrace with the droll disapproval which is the stock response to a homosexual advance. As the duo move offstage left, Spiderman motions behind his back, snapping his yo-yo up and down masterfully.

The lights dim quickly to black and come up with Spiderman appearing at a ceremonial procession led by a figure at once religious and military. The figure wears a floor-length white gown embroidered with purple and gold, and a high-peaked hat. But his staff, which knocks against the ground in an audience-silencing rhythm, is topped by a brilliant twisted brass spider, which a spotlight emblazons. Spotlights all about the night-lighted stage then create a strobe effect, which dizzies and hypnotizes the audience.

An apparent wedding takes place with Spiderman in the role of the bride's father, and the play dramatically ends as bells ring and the bride and groom buzz at one another in a sexual fever. A telephone's insistent ringing is also heard.

The play, as history has it, was forced to close after only one performance by an enraged group of cultural guardians. And the playwright, accosted at a favorite café, was badly beaten, the fingers of his left, his writing hand, individually broken. The script itself vanished, and only Brezina's notes recount the essentials of the performance. But most remarkable (if true), the play as recorded by Brezina was a clear-cut, prescient representation of events that were to occur a full sixteen months later! The author was beaten by a gang of brownshirts celebrating the Reichstag fire of 1933, and the play appeared whole to him as a vision in his hospital bed.

With the energy of a religious zealot, he saw to it that a production was mounted. Following a six-month prison sentence for the sale of furniture he did not own, he was hounded from Germany before a second play, *Colibri*, was performed. In 1935, he founded the well-known religious order that bears his name to this day.

*

In reality, we know also that a telephone did dramatically and insistently ring in the Hotel Kaiserhof in Essen on the Thursday night of June 28, 1934. And that Karl Ernst, a key Stormtrooper leader from Berlin, had been the groom at an extraordinary wedding ceremony which included Chancellor Hitler and other high-ranking Nazis. It was at this Essen wedding that Hitler had been targeted for assassination, though a suspicious pastry chef warned the SS, and the plot was thwarted several days earlier.

Horst Dörner, one of Hitler's bodyguards on this wedding trip, heard the phone ring all night long. Later he saw messenger Paul Korner (a friend of Göring's) arrive to tell Hitler in person about an "imminent" Stormtrooper uprising, an uprising that the German Army (General von Reichenau) greatly feared. On Hitler's orders, Horst was sent back with others to Berlin to alert his fellows in the SS Leibstandarte. Hitler phoned Röhm, who was vacationing in the south, lakeside, and arranged a meeting with the head Stormtroop leader for Saturday, the 30th.

Horst arrived in Berlin in the early morning hours of Friday, the 29th. Following a typically early breakfast, he attended to his official responsibilities, then called his girl (Lisel Ganz) to make a date for lunch. The wedding, prototypically Aryan, had been a special inspiration to him, and his last dream before waking had been rich with meaning.

CHAPTER THIRTEEN

BY the next morning, Friday the 29th, a two-day storm had come and gone. The black clouds that had gathered on Wednesday, the high winds and damp air, had burst, drenching the streets of Berlin, deafening the Berliners with Thor's thunder. The rain had brought no relief, no cooler air behind it. Instead, the atmosphere was closer than before. The sun was like a fire heating a cauldron; one could see waves of heat rippling around the black rims of roofs.

All morning, Albert sat in his living room in shirt-sleeves. At least the pang was gone from the butt of his right arm. It was not cooler in the high-ceilinged white room. He was sitting on the pale grey couch, a newspaper lying beside him. He had sent Lotte away, "on holiday" to the south where her people lived. Lisel had gone out "on errands." (He suspected, in fact, it was to see her Nazi.) The apartment was like a tomb, empty save for the growing, gnawing heat.

A morning for sad memories, his father had called times like these after Albert's mother had died, and indeed, Albert recalled the dozens of high-spirited battles that had raged in this room—the tables crowded with bottles, the sofas and chairs with the old companions waving their hands, gesturing, posturing, sometimes Konrad in the midst of it, or Ludvik, or even himself.

The heat of the day pressed in. He missed her, oddly, of all things, though she'd only be gone for the day. Of all the people to be left with and to need in such a fundamental way, a nineteen-year-old girl who cried in her sleep. He recalled how Hilde had cried when he'd left her for the War—though she had, at least, understood—unlike his father, the old cynic, for whom "national honor" was a cunning illusion by which the rich and powerful furthered their interests at the expense of the young and congenitally ignorant. "Hitler, coming from the ranks of the Army, is and always will be one of us!" proclaimed an Army spokesman in the *Völkisher Beobachter*, the newspaper that lay beside Albert. The news, like the heat, grew worse by the day.

Small rivers and estuaries of sweat formed on his body; his neck and thighs prickled with the heat. He had sat motionless for so long that moving in the oppressive swelter seemed a near impossibility, but momentarily and for no apparent reason, a sigh escaped his lips and he rose. (Perhaps the pigeon by the window had caught his eye.) He left the room, slowly climbed the stairs, and found himself, as he had for the last several days, going to Lisel's bedroom for a solitary visit. In a sense it was the last room in the apartment where life still bloomed. Possibly that was his tie to the girl, too, he thought; she was the last intimate connection to his past life, and unlike himself, she continued to build her days with aims and directions. There was also, he knew, though he couldn't say it, another connection, one as uncomplicated and inevitable as the summer heat. The white skin that glistened on the back of her legs was one of its several inspirations. Her mouth that in sleep was pouted and moist was another. Tuesday, when she'd held him as he cried over Konrad, was the start. The next morning he passed her room, the door to which was half-open, and looked in. She had just slipped off the summer nightie he had given her. Naked, she turned to face him, sensing his presence.

"How do you feel?" she asked without modesty.

"Better," he nodded.

"I shall be down in a few moments; I am hungry today."

"Good," he said inanely.

The puff below her belly was as blond as her hair. Her nipples, in contrast, were ripe with color. She was an Aryan princess with a spirit made "Jewish" by the very people who ought to have worshipped her. And her sufferings had been Job-like. Like himself, in a peculiar way, she was a kind of *Mischlinge*, like a daughter or sister. But as he left for the kitchen, the image of her hand slowly rising to cover her breasts, for her an after-thought, was a provocative reminder that his feelings for her were more than familial. At breakfast, like a university student, he followed droplets of sweat that ran down her neck and disappeared below her pink blouse under the curve of her breasts. Her voice sounded to him like a violin. When the rain came, he wanted to take her by the hand and stand with her in it till their clothes were soaked through.

For dignity's sake, he restrained himself, and instead, after a morning of low feverish talk, he pressed into her hand a brooch he had gotten for Hilde on their honeymoon, though he had said nothing about its origins and she accepted it only for the day. And the offering and the acceptance worked a marvelous transformation on him, cooled him off, so to speak. On Thursday, when he successfully resisted her return of the brooch, their relationship moved to another plane, a kind of special intimacy, he believed, that soothed more than it excited, though for the first time in years he experienced the pangs of jealousy when she referred or even alluded to her Nazi.

He looked at the cosmetics table on the wall across from her bed. The comb and brush as always were together on the right, the bottles of perfume and cologne to the left. When he turned, there was something wrong about the night table, however. On it was a book, of all things, and an oddly familiar one at that. He went to the table and picked the volume up. It was a little treatise Konrad and he had debated at the university over twenty years ago. Yes, all to do with the great-man theory of history and the probable consequences that certain timely assassinations would have produced. What possible meaning could a book like this have for Lisel?

An answer was quick in coming, for as soon as he opened the pages, he found a half-finished letter in Lisel's rounded script, a sad little note to her mother tucked into a middle chapter. Albert nodded. She had used the book as a tablet on which to write the letter, he decided, and had probably not read even the first word of it. Poor Lisel. He well understood the sadness of a child whose parent cannot or will not understand her.

The book brought back memories as he held it. What

debates it had engendered! It was, no doubt of it, a bizarre analysis that had swept through the university like a brushfire. Its author was and remained unknown, an eccentric who had only written this one work, but the speculations were, as Albert read them through again, peculiarly interesting and persuasive, particularly those about Napoleon, which a young Konrad had decorated with many enthusiastic commentaries. For Konrad at the time, the book had nearly become a fifth gospel. And, in fact, as recently as April, Konrad had referred to one of its examples to illustrate a point he was making about Hitler.

Those university years were very special to Albert, his last days of innocence—though it was also during this period that he married Hilde. Two Germans meeting in Venice, and he wearing that preposterous Alpine chapeau! Compared to the careful girls with whom he was familiar, Hilde was irresistible. She was four years his senior, traveled alone, lectured irrepressibly on the dangers of repression, and when she found that Albert painted, she quickly enlisted her own services as a model and critic. She counted her father, a professor of history, among the wisest men in Germany, and found everyone else, except herself, immensely amusing.

When Albert needed a nude, she accepted the challenge with characteristic bravado, for though she was classically handsome, a birth defect, a large red-and-purple macula, ran across her stomach under her heart. Oddly, there was no other spot or mole on any part of her, and the blemish proved, she said, that there was either no God, or that if there were one, He was Jewish—since the hideous mark was by any *human* estimation, undeserved. Albert regarded the inky tattoo with horror. She challenged him to include it in the painting, but he shrouded it in darkness. Art, he explained, was not a recreation of life, but of the artist's perceptions. In a later painting, he included the mark, but as the crimson shadow of a bird that was a manifestation of a secret desire. They were married in July of 1914 on his twenty-first birthday. It was, up till then, the happiest moment of his life.

Albert settled down onto Lisel's bed and lay back. He closed his eyes, and as frequently happened in this dream, Hilde slipped into bed with him, her low voice rousing him to the drowsy wakefulness of a Sunday.

"We have a little visitor this morning."

"And who is that?" he said, though he was cradling a small bundle in the bend of his arm and studying Gerta's little face with fatherly adoration.

"I think today she looks like her grandpapa," Hilde teased.

"She looks like her beautiful mama."

Hilde giggled. She was naked under the sheets, and her smooth skin rubbed against his own. He slid his hand over her breasts. She sighed and stretched her hands towards the headboard, in the pose of a Renoir bather. His hand moved over her belly and inside the curve of her thigh. His mouth found the lustrous hollow of her shoulder and neck. In the dim light, the dark macula was a coral lake, the skin of it water-smooth and warm. With typical enthusiasm, she lifted her breast to his mouth.

At a distance, Gerta was crawling on a blanket spread with picnic foods. Then in Hilde's arms she formed a shimmering portrait with her mother, of light and green and gold. He took the baby in his own arms, and Hilde smiled. Together, they walked through a park along the Spree, which was the amber that appeared in so many of his paintings.

In his last scene of her, she was reclining on the divan in his studio, posing for him in a satin gown, her hair tucked up in ringlets around her face. She lifted her hand to her lips as if she had forgotten something, then she grew dark with light, and he was awake, staring at the white ceiling above him.

He bent forward to prolong the illusion of the dream by focusing on a painting that hung on the far wall. It was one he had done himself, the first he had done after the War, of Hilde and Gerta, the child on the lap of her mother. When he had done it, Konrad suggested he create the scene from memory, as a therapy to relieve himself of his paralyzing grief. Remarkably, it had worked, and in the end, the loss of his wife and daughter to the epidemic of '18 had left only an invisible macula over his own heart, which for many years passed for wisdom. His left hand also ceased its rebellion in those difficult weeks of forebearance and struggle—even though now, on occasion, it was a stranger to him (for like his father, he resisted change, even after it had occurred). Refusal to accept the facts was a defect he must control, he thought, particularly at times like these. (Or was this a warning Ludvik had given him?)

Albert rose to leave, and a puzzle flowered in his mind.

He remembered that he had last seen the book on Konrad's table in the rectory. How then had it gotten here? Of course, Konrad could have brought it, he reasoned. But when? And why? Least plausible: Lisel had been to Konrad's rooms and taken it with her. Or was he even mistaken about where he'd last seen it? He descended the stairs for the cold glass of tea that waited in the kitchen. And if she had read it, what of it?

The east-facing kitchen was darkening. As he entered it, another more acute worry arose: Konrad. Was he alive? Where? Ironically, under circumstances like these, it was Konrad he would talk to. In fact, Albert had told no one of his deepest concerns. He had told no one of his visit to Konrad's rectory on the day after his disappearance.

Then, he had strolled several kilometers to the northwest, on the lively streets by the Philharmonic Hall, then two blocks east to the immaculate grey-stone church. Though it was his friend's custom to leave the large wooden doors open, today they were closed. Thinking little of this, he climbed the steps in the smaller, northern wing to Konrad's lodgings.

The door to the apartment was open—another oddity—and inside, the room was in shambles. The momentary smile at his friend's slovenliness vanished in a surge of understanding and anxiety. The books were strewn about. Konrad's chair was smashed. Even the pillow on which his friend slept had been razored and thrown to the floor. The note hidden between the old moulding and the door where Konrad often left messages for Albert was distressing and brief: *I am lost to you. Do not come looking.*

"Hey, *you*!" someone had shouted at him from below.

"*You there*!" another voice yelled, drawing closer. Two faces appeared at the base of the stairway.

"I am looking for the Father." Albert knew the smell of danger.

"For what? "

"I am a parishoner," he said with authority. He pushed the note into his pocket, but the movement was detected.

"What are you doing up there?"

"Nothing." He began to descend.

"Get down here." They waited for him on the landing. His descent was deliberate and slow.

"What's in your pocket?"

"My pocket?"

The larger of the two—though neither was large—reached into Albert's pocket and found the note. Albert recognized the black uniforms of the SS.

"It's nothing important," he said casually.

"What's this?"

"It's a prayer," he lied.

"A prayer?"

"It's in Latin." His blood shed ice.

"What's the matter?"

"I am not feeling well." A spasm surged through his abdomen.

"What is your name?"

"Ganz."

"What?" The larger was writing.

"Ganz," he lied again.

The smaller one eyed him curiously.

"May we see your papers, Herr Ganz?" said the larger.

"My papers? Yes, I suppose you may."

The muscles in his neck had contracted into a battery of fear, yet he drew himself up, and reached into his jacket for his billfold and the identity papers which would betray him.

"Apologies for my ..."

"Of course," said the larger, noticing for the first time the suspect's missing right hand. "You served?" he asked with some interest.

"Yes," Albert smiled. "You may call it that... at the Somme." He said this telegraphically and with meaning. "If you are familiar with the '18' offensive."

"Yes," the larger one nodded.

The smaller one, whose father had been a tailor, now observed the cut and expensive buttons of the suspect's summer suit, then the blue tie which was silk and the white handkerchief that formed three small peaks above the breast pocket. The brown alligator billford appeared in the left hand and a flick of the wrist opened it like a book. The smaller one's eyes were magnetized by a folio of hundred-mark bills.

The larger one was impressed, but confused.

"Yes?" Albert said.

"I see no papers, Herr Ganz."

In a moment of incredulity and sudden understanding, unrevealed in even the smallest twitch of muscle, Albert had realized there could be no papers. Not in this billfold at any rate. For the documents, in fact, lay on the large bureau in his room, where he'd neglected to transfer them to this, his new billfold, because of Lisel's incessant chirping all morning long about of all subjects, Napoleon Bonaparte. (There were moments, he had sworn at the time, that she hadn't changed a gram from the empty-headed model he first met. *Bless her*!)

"I've apparently left my papers at home," he said with careful restraint. Then, "Perhaps some of these papers will do as well," he heard himself say. "Please," he continued, "for the service you perform and for which we all, as true Germans, are more than grateful." He pushed a half dozen notes forward with his thumb. "Unless, of course, I insult your honor."

"On the contrary," said the larger.

Again his bowels surged, and he flinched imperceptibly.

"Heil Hitler," the smaller one said after taking his share.

"Heil Hitler," Albert repeated with drama.

He nodded, turned with military precision, and walked away in a slow and confident gait. Surely they would come for him in a moment, he thought. Surely in a moment—but he turned the corner unchallenged and vanished.

At the church, the officers wondered briefly at the suspect's apparent unconcern with the priest's overturned room, and the larger folded the "prayer" into a black book. Each had been instructed to exercise tact and circumspection following the Marburg speech. Moreover, as those who worship personality, they were overmatched by the suspect's dignity and authority.

"There, Heinrich, goes a *German* gentleman," the larger had said.

His companion nodded, sniffing again the rankness in

the air which he attributed to his colleague's inability to digest cabbage and sausage. Certainly the putrid air was no doing of a gentleman who dressed and spoke so well. In reality, of course, it was the lingering remnant of Albert's fear—and the only honest information he had given them.

He thought he heard someone at the door.

"Lisel?" he called out too loudly.

But there was no reply.

It had been several days since they'd had the note, and ample time to see it was not prayer. His use of Lisel's surname in place of his own was a source of shame to him, and he was convinced that she knew what he'd done though she said nothing about it. Yet Albert had learned over the years that silence allows one's mind to reshape certain events into acceptable form. And no consequences had radiated from the confrontation at the church thus far.

Now he carefully rinsed his glass, set the pitcher of tea into the ice box, and made for the stairs and his studio to resume his work. His art. Surely Konrad knew he would not have looked, that he lacked the courage. Had he ever had courage? Had it been a sign of cowardice to lie to the Gestapo? The truth would have accomplished nothing, except to jeopardize his own well-being for no purpose. But to give Lisel's name, and thereby to jeopardize her? Had he more time, he would have given another name—invented another. In fact, to give her name was not a shameful act, but the result of having to make a quick decision—nothing more, nothing less.

Albert squeezed a mound of white onto his palette. All

afternoon, in silence he created and recreated history like this. All afternoon he listened for Lisel's return.

During the same time, three hundred and fifty kilometers to the west, Hitler was visiting Labor Service camps in Westphalia as Göring and Himmler continued to whisper in his ear that armed bands of Stormtroopers were marching through Berlin. A coup, they insisted, led by Ernest Röhm, would begin at four p.m. on Saturday. Hitler went to rest late in the day at an old crony's hotel in Godesberg, where Goebbels met him and told Hitler that Karl Ernst, the Essen newlywed, had also alerted his Berlin Stormtroopers.

"I've had enough!" Hitler screamed. "I shall make an *example of them*!"

CHAPTER FOURTEEN

THAT night when Lisel returned to the apartment, she found Mr. Entrater upstairs, painting. The record cabinet was loudly playing. Yet there was no smell of alcohol in the studio—though beyond the paint and turpentine, she did not know if she could smell drink. The artist was working, however, as if he were quite drunk. It occurred to her that she had never watched him paint before. When she had modeled for him (in another life, it seemed), she had daydreamed so he had had to scold her into readopting her pose. Since she had moved in, she had learned how private he was about his work. In fact, when she came upon him, she did not know if she should even interrupt to tell him she was back. He seemed to know she was there without speech, however. Without turning to face her, he spoke over the music.

"How goes the future of the Reich?"

She was close enough to him that he could smell a hint of the French perfume he had given her. He stopped work, holding up a brush thick with red paint. He looked at her. She was dressed in a blue dress with a full skirt. There was white embroidery around the sleeves, and her waist was outlined by a white belt. Hilde's brooch was on the blue collar.

"The news is good," she said.

He nodded. He was painting Seigfried's fallen cloak. She tilted her head to examine his work. He went to the phonograph and turned down the music, then resumed his position at the easel.

"He looks like Father Konrad," she said, pointing to Seigfried in the wet painting.

"How's your Nazi?" he asked.

"He's invited me to a tea party at the Chancellery. For Sunday afternoon. He cannot live without me."

Albert glanced over his shoulder, caught the strange look in her eyes. "Yes. It is Konrad," he said.

She sat down on a green leather chair, folded her hands carefully, like a pigeon settling its wings. Then she made a similar point of putting her feet together. He felt her behind him, but forced himself to concentrate on the painting. He was taller than Horst, she decided, and broader-shouldered. Like Uncle Karl. She thought of all the things she had not noticed about him before. There was paint on the back of his hand, which was not hairy. She disliked hairy hands and forearms and Horst's narrowness. She and Horst looked together like the figures that once came out of clocks to tell the weather. It was still warm in the studio. It was warm everywhere. She unbuttoned the collar of her dress. She looked at the eyes of the man in the painting, who resembled Father Konrad, then upwards on the canvas to another man with a bloody sword. He looked both afraid and proud of the murder he had done. She stared into the murderer's eyes and then the eyes of all the others standing beyond him in the woods—there was a stream in the foreground, reddening with blood. The eyes frightened her. She twisted in her chair and unclasped her hands. She had the beginning of that awful feeling again. She stood, began to pace about. When she spoke, she heard her own voice as if it belonged to someone else. She saw a hummingbird (*Colibri*!) tremble before her eyes. He turned. She hated the concern she saw on his face.

"I didn't spend the whole day with him," she said. "He had to fly somewhere. By aeroplane! Later I went to the cinema."

"Are you all right?"

"He wants to marry me," she said. "We are facing some crisis."

"What crisis?"

"I don't know," she lied.

He stroked on red paint.

"It was an old film they had." She paused. "A girl tried to save her fiance by giving up the life of another. But when she saved an infant in a burning hospital, she wouldn't give up the baby to save her fiance. And she died in the fire herself. At the end, the two ghosts, she and her fiance, stood at the top of a hill, and you could see the sky through them."

He changed brushes. "Lang's *Destiny.* "

"Yes." She held her white handkerchief. "Horst says the days of shame and betrayal will soon be over. He was talking about the flags being at half-mast yesterday. Because of the Versailles Treaty fifteen years ago. The treaty makes his scar go all white." She touched her cheek with a fingertip. "He tells me about a wedding he went to in Essen. He was with the Führer and Karl Ernst, who is a Stormtroop leader in Berlin."

Albert dipped the white brush into a metallic mixture. He made waves appear in the stream; they broke by Seigfried's pale face. She saw it happen and still couldn't believe it. There was magic in his brush. She could feel the wind that ruffled the stream although she could see it was caused by no more than several strokes from the brush he held in his hand.

"He meant to impress me," she said.

"Arsonists might impress you then." He glanced at her quickly. "It was Ernst who lit the Reichstag fire." He referred to the burning of the German legislature in 1933, the symbolic end of German democracy. He dabbed on some paint, then stroked it smooth.

"I must tell you something," her voice was very low. "I'm pregnant."

He put down his brush. He wiped his hand expertly with a steamy turpentine cloth, then put it down.

"I also asked about Father Konrad," she said. "He told me to put that Catholic right out of my mind because Catholics are no better than Jews because they worship one. He started describing how our wedding would be like the new Aryan ceremony from Essen."

"Is that what he said by way of comfort?"

She placed her hand on the topmost book in the stack on the table beside her, the Christie mystery that Albert and Konrad had shared. She became quite suddenly still.

He noticed the pause, then the familiar look. Her eyes were glassy. He watched images flickering inside her mind; then her eyes darted about as if she were sleeping.

His voice came to her from a distance though his arm was around her like a band of iron. He pressed her against himself, and there was the comforting paint-smell of his shirt and the beating of his heart. She pressed against him to get closer to the sound. Then there was silence.

When she opened her eyes, she was in her bedroom. He was drying his hand on a towel. The violet clusters on the white wallpaper looked real. He sat down on the needle-point chair and rubbed his hand against his thigh.

"Are you feeling better?"

"Yes, I think."

"That was a record-breaker."

"I am thirsty."

He handed her the ready glass of water.

"Thank you."

"Tell me." He hesitated.

"Yes?

"You are pregnant since when? Since May?"

"Yes. I'm sorry, I shouldn't have told you—"

"The Stormtroopers?"

"Yes."

He spoke calmly. "We must act quickly, Lisel."

She shook her head. "I know what I must do."

"You must let me help."

"I am tired."

"Listen to me—"

"Please."

The humidity made his face glisten. "Is this why you are marrying him?"

"I will be all right."

"That is no *reason*," he persisted. "Do you *understand* that?"

"Tomorrow I must leave here for good. And you must also leave tomorrow. For Amsterdam. You will find Father Konrad. He will help you, and you will be safe."

"How will I find Father Konrad?"

"I don't know."

"You have seen this?"

"Yes."

"You have also seen me dead."

"Yes."

"Have you seen this just now?"

"In part."

"And how will I be *safe*?"

"I don't know, not *precisely*."

"You have seen me dead. A man cannot have two destinies."

"You don't know!"

He rose from the chair and sat beside her on the bed. "Please." She drew back.

He examined her face from which all the colors of the bruises had faded into a rosy cream, like strawberry milk one nanny used to make for him in a summer long ago. Only one still-red scar crossed one of her fine eyebrows. He could tell that in time it would become as light as her hair. One day it would look like a wind-blown strand almost touching her eyes. Someone would reach to push it out of the way. "Stay with me," he said. "Be here with me."

She shook her head. "I cannot."

"Why?"

"You will have to leave the country. Because of Horst… because of *me*… that is how your generosity is being repaid."

"I am in *love* with you." His high voice broke.

He pulled her to himself. Her face burned through his shirt into his skin. Her own neck glistened with sweat. Against his chest, she heard his harsh breath through the rushing waters in her ears. She pressed against him, raising her head up to his shoulder, then lifted up her face. Before she spoke, he kissed her. She could feel the heat and moisture of *his* skin now, the sudden wetness of his mouth. Fear swept through her. Through the pounding of his ears, Albert heard her cry out.

He stopped.

His eyes were wide, unblinking. Despair flowered in him. First he felt it for her, and then he felt it for himself. And the despair reshaped itself into dread. It spread through him like a stain. She reached for his hand and held it. Her mouth half-open, she leaned toward him, kissed him. But he rose, though she continued to grip his hand. He stood beside the bed and looked at her. Her eyes were filled with tears. She unclasped his hand.

"I am sorry." She looked up at him.

"Yes."

"You must go"

"I am so sorry," he said. "I am."

"Tomorrow."

"Yes," he said.

He felt her eyes X-ray him, delineate the cage of his ribs and the tiny bird that fluttered inside—his soul, his pathetic chirping little soul. He did not hear her last words as he left the room.

He shut the bedroom door, already in his mind packing clothes in a valise. When he went to the window in his own bedroom to breathe some cooler air—had there ever been such a hot summer in such a high latitude?—there was no cool air to breathe and there was no moon. All the planets that had been all winter in the morning sky now were evening stars. And outside in the parks of Berlin it was another warm June night, full of many moistures and the amorous fireflies.

CHAPTER FIFTEEN

THE next day, Saturday the 30th, he awoke much later than usual, feeling drugged. His eyes were heavy, his shoulders sluggish with the anesthesia of sleep. His first thought was of her, and he put his robe on and went into the hallway. The apartment was silent. He called her name, but there was no reply. He peered down the stairs, listened another moment, then went to her room, which was empty—vacated, actually. The perfumes, colognes, and brushes were gone. The drawers were empty. In the closet, only two dresses were left—two dresses which had, in fact, been Hilde's. There were no wrinkles in the made-up bed, no doilies on the chairs; not even the scent he had become familiar with remained.

"Good morning," Lisel said quietly.

He turned, and incredibly she was there. "I thought you'd gone," he said.

"Almost."

"I slept in."

"Yes."

She was wearing the dress she'd arrived in three weeks earlier.

"What time is it?" he asked.

"Nearly eleven."

"I've decided to stay," he said. "Regardless."

She shook her head. "I am leaving in half an hour. I will help you pack."

"I am not going."

She made no reply.

"I will dress and we will talk about it then."

"All right," she said.

"Things are never so bad as they seem," he said. He inhaled her fragrance. "You smell delicious."

"Thank you." Like a girl, she averted her eyes.

"I haven't slept so long since I was a student."

She smiled.

When he entered the bathroom, a white chill ran through him. His back began to ache, and his neck. He stopped by the tub and an anxiety gripped him. He called her name.

"Yes?" she answered.

"Despite the heat, I am hungry for a real breakfast!" Albert called.

"Yes," she repeated.

He stretched again to awaken his body, rotated his head to unstiffen his cracking neck and shoulders. It had been a decade, more, since he had slept and awakened like a young man. In his mind, the past evening and abortive seduction were under desperate revision. But at the mirror, the truth reappeared: the face stared back from the cloudy glass, the watery eyes, the wisps of hair, the skin like a pastry wrapping. He examined his tongue with middle-aged concern, then the pink suffusion in his eyes. He had once seen his own father at a mirror in the same comical pose—in his "second youth" and on the verge of his second marriage. Yet Albert was only forty; his father had been… his father had been forty-five. Meager comfort in that.

Lisel's face appeared in the mirror.

"Are you all right?"

"Oh, yes," he said.

She stood in the doorway. "I think you must hurry."

"Yes."

"You will be all right."

He nodded. "I'll be done in a moment," he said. Then he went about his business, the last minutes he would ever spend in this bath. He washed his teeth, shaved—scratched himself with the old razor; his new one was gone. When he entered the room, his small overnight valise had been packed. A large open valise lay on the made-up bed. Before he could speak, Lisel did.

"Have you your passport?"

"Yes," he said.

"Where?"

"In the drawer."

She opened the bureau and found it.

"You have enough money?"

"Yes."

"I have taken all my things," she said.

"Where?"

"They have been disposed of."

"Lisel."

Downstairs there was someone at the door.

"It is my taxi," she said. "Thank you."

"Wait."

"God bless you. Be very careful." She kissed him, then left.

He did not pursue her. Instead, he listened to her vanishing footsteps, then stood by the window and watched her enter the black cab with her small suitcase and her purse. The car drove away, north, toward Motz Street. He watched it disappear into shadow. In his drawer he found a clean shirt. He selected a light tan suit from the closet and his cordovan walking shoes. He slipped on his watch, tucked his billfold and passport into his breast pocket, filled his left trouser pocket with extra bills in a silver money clip. He decided to leave the change on the dresser.

Outside, he heard a car pull up, the metal doors open and close. He went to the window. It was the Gestapo. Two men approached his front door. He stood motionless and considered the causes and the implications. Time both accelerated and slowed. Downstairs, the bell rang. They had translated the so-called prayer, but he had not given his name. Perhaps it was Lisel they wanted. Why? His link to Konrad, of course, was a factor. Important not to appear frightened. Important not to run. But the dark hole at 8 Prinz Albrechtstrasse… the door from the kitchen opened onto a back garden through which he might pass to Grunewald Street. Downstairs, the bell rang insistently. He would not go for his auto. The presence of the auto might keep them at the house just long enough. He picked up the small packed valise and descended the stairs, through the halls he would never see again, into Lotte's kitchen, then out the door, as quietly as possible. The door had swollen with the high humidity; he could not shut it without a thud. He left it ajar and then he was gone, through the walk of red and yellow flowers and the shaped bushes. Soon, he was on Grunewald walking east.

Grunewald intersected with Bambergerstrasse. He best chance was to hail a cab as soon as possible and take it to the train station. A cab, however, appeared even sooner than he hoped, traveling west on Grunewald. Yet he was only twenty or thirty meters from his house, and in hailing it, he would run a double risk: that his voice would be heard, and then that the cab would drive past the corner of Grunewald and Prinzregenstrasse only meters from his house and the parked SS sedan. He decided he could ask the driver to take him to the railroad yards, which would force the taxi south on Prinzregenstrasse, away from his house. He never got the chance. A sharp voice halted him from behind.

"Herr Entrater!"

He might still make a dash for the taxi, but he was frozen in the hot air.

"Herr Entrater, if you please!"

The taxi driver, a white-faced man, looked at the well-dressed gentleman and the SS officer at the corner.

"Herr Entrater, if you please!" The officer gripped his arm like a vise. The cab sped away to the west.

"Here!" called the officer to his compatriot at Albert's door. "I have him!"

"What is all this?" he asked calmly. But he received

no answer. Soon they were driving north to 8 Prinz Albrechtstrasse, the greystone SS headquarters.

The streets of the city were sluggish with the heat. At a glittery corner of Kurfurstendamm, a brown tomcat darted among cars and pedestrians, chased by a black-and-white mongrel, which was knocked sideways by a taxi accelerating for a fare, but everyone else moved in slow motion. At Augsberger Street, two boys escorted a grey-haired woman across. She is their grandmother, he thought, until on the far side she gave them each a coin and they ran off laughing. In the dark interior, street sounds and humid wind contributed to the restive stillness. The pink-faced officers sweated in their starched collars and black wool jackets. By the journey's end, he was also wet under his arms and back with perspiration. He considered the reasons for this apprehension, what he would do under various circumstances, how much he could safely afford to lie, how much he could safely afford to reveal. He was genuinely ignorant, though that was not always a guarantee. He felt oddly calm, as when anxiety gives way to action. At the door of 8 Prinz Albrechtstrasse, he was nearly confident.

A black-eyed officer greeted him from behind a large desk in a small office. A hawk-faced secretary in a black skirt and white blouse left the room.

"Herr Entrater?"

"Yes."

"Sorry to bother you."

"That is all right."

The desk was piled with papers. "We are under some

strain today." He rose, gesturing to a chair for Albert to sit. "We have asked you here for confirmation."

"Confirmation?" He sat and folded his hands.

"Confirmation is the essence of our trade."

"Yes."

"Are you traveling?" He regarded the overnight bag that Albert had laid beside him.

"I am going south," he lied. "To visit an old family friend." He gave Lotte's address in Bavaria.

"It is good to have friends who live where it is cool."

He nodded with a smile.

"A friend for how long?"

"A woman who helped raise me."

"A 'friend'?"

"Yes."

"Very democratic. Fraulein Gotz, you mean."

"Yes." It was Lotte's surname. Albert smiled.

"Are you acquainted with Herr Konrad Hoeffer?"

"Yes."

"For how long?"

"Since childhood."

"A lifelong friend?"

He nodded.

"And Herr Erich Weiss?"

"Only an acquaintance."

"A friendly acquainance?"

"Not especially." He remembered a tall redhead who spouted Bakunin at every opportunity, a self-styled anarchist, whom Konrad was forever in the process of redeeming.

"There is no advantage to lying."

"I am not lying."

"Excuse me." Another voice said. Then a face appeared in the doorway. "Have you seen Colonel Kostler?"

"He is at Stadelheirn with the others." It was the larger of the officers who had stopped Albert at the church, the one whom he'd given Konrad's 'prayer.'

He nodded to Albert perfunctorily. "Good morning."

"Good morning."

"How does it go?" the visitor asked his colleague.

"We've arrested a hundred, more or less. Röhm has been taken, to Munich."

The visitor was looking at Albert intently now. As best he could, Albert concealed his missing hand.

"I am going with Haller," the visitor said. He looked again at Albert and smiled. "Haller is frothing at the mouth."

"As ever. Come, Herr Entrater." Albert reached for his bag. "Leave your things."

They moved to the door.

"Heil Hitler."

"Heil Hitler."

"Heil Hitler." Albert added.

"Come this way."

Albert accompanied the black-eyed officer down the hall; then they descended metal stairs. The air below ground was damp and cool. They walked down another hallway in dim light. Three brownshirt officers were engaged in animated conversation. An SS guard stood beside them. They turned with a start toward an opening door, then entered a yellow-lit room as Albert walked by.

"You do seem busy today."

"We are cleaning house for the Führer. Some of our colleagues have lost sight of our agenda," Albert's escort said.

Their heels clicked on the stone floor.

"Understand, Herr Entrater, we are interested only in the truth. About that we are very particular."

"Yes."

"No one is larger than the Reich."

They had walked, he surmised, to one end of the building. There was a dismal smell in the air, a rankness. The black-eyed officer found keys, slipped one into the keyhole of a green door.

"Are you squeamish?"

"I don't?"

They entered a windowless square room. In it were a wooden desk and chair, three facing chairs, and a boy-faced guard to one side of a grey door on the left wall. In front of the guard, their backs to him, on Albert's left as he entered, were Erich Weiss and Konrad.

They sat straight up, bound in hard-back chairs, Weiss to the right, Konrad to the left. The middle chair was yet empty. As the officer sat down behind the desk, he gestured Albert to step forward, then stopped him, standing, by raising his wide palm. Then Albert glanced to see that Weiss's red hair had been crudely shaved from one side of his scalp, which was mottled with yellow blisters and pink burns. His nose was swollen and one of his ears was wrapped in a blood-marked gauze. His pale eyes stared straight ahead. Konrad, on first glance, was comparatively uninjured, and Albert was relieved, until he noticed the swollen black pits in each hand and the same through the top arch of each bare foot. He was wearing his clerical black and white, a parody of the Nazi colors, but the collar was loose and there were several sutures at his throat over a small mound of red flesh, such as where a tracheotomy might be performed, or several centimeters above. Unlike Weiss's, his eyes were responsive to Albert. His mouth, tightly shut, puckered, but he made no sound.

"Unfortunately, circumstances have required a surgical procedure to restore the Father's voice, but his vocal cords have been severed in the process. Now he only *whispers* to us." The officer smiled.

Still standing, Albert said, "I see." He noticed Konrad's lips, which trembled, and the tightening muscles of his jaw.

The officer regarded the vacant-eyed anarchist. "Herr Weiss alleges he was with you and Father Konrad on the evening of May 25th at a party at your home. If this is true, it may clear both Herr Weiss and the Father of particular charges. It is, therefore, to their advantage that you should confirm this allegation… of course, the confirmation might implicate you as well."

Albert remembered the "book-burning" party, the editor's wife, the bald jokester.

"Do you care to know the charges?"

Albert hesitated.

"Conspiracy to assassinate the Chancellor."

He looked at the black-eyed officer.

"So you see, we want the truth. *All* of it."

Weiss turned toward him and moaned. Then Albert looked back at Konrad, who returned the stare. Albert knew there was no escape for either. Only his own future hung in the balance. But in what respect? A harsh exhalation caught his attention. It was Konrad shaking his head at him, warning him. The black-eyed officer struck Konrad a sudden blow, and the priest slumped forward like a ragdoll. Albert's blood surged. Despite the consequences, he must lie for his friend, make some kind of stand. Or fight back even.

Yet when he spoke, barely audible, he denied them both.

"Quite certain?" asked the officer.

"Yes." He nodded. "Quite certain."

There was silence.

"Never there?"

"No."

The officer smiled. "Why don't I believe you?"

"It's quite true."

"Empty your pockets, Herr Entrater," he said quietly. "Empty them."

The words echoed. Albert's ears pounded. He obeyed.

"I don't understand."

The officer pointed. "*This* is what I do not understand."

"It is my passport."

"For a trip to *Bavaria*?" The officer waited.

"I intend to visit Italy next, Venice—"

"No, you do *not*."

"Yes—"

"You are a Jew?"

"I am a *half* Jew."

"And what is your *name*?"

"My name is Entrater."

"Not *Ganz*?"

"Ganz?"

Of course they knew. The larger officer from the church had come by to confirm it.

"The name you gave Monday, claiming then to be a Catholic."

"You must be mistaken."

"Sit down." He obeyed. "You are up to your eyes in this matter."

"No—"

He jammed his hand under Albert's jaw, forced his thumb like a pincer under his ear, then snapped his head. Albert attempted to rise, but the heel of the officers hand came down at the bridge of his nose and he was blinded. He whimpered in pain.

"You are *finished* now!"

The hand came across his face like a whip.

"But I *swear*!"

The heel of a boot cracked his knee.

"No!" At first he felt nothing. Then again the boot, and pain, like volts of electricity, tore at his leg. He lay bent double to cradle it, protect it. The clenched fist came down across his neck, knocking him to the ground. He looked up at the black-clad legs, desperate. He shook his head. "I tell you I know *nothing*."

The boot kicked him over, sideways, like a despised animal. He panted, sprawled on the cold floor.

"Get up."

"Please."

"Get up."

"I can't."

"You will *confess* now, like your *friends*."

"But I am *innocent*." Albert could not see from his left eye. He reached up to touch it, afraid of what he'd find. There was wetness on his fingers, and blood. The young guard looked on with poorly concealed fascination. "Believe me, please," said Albert.

"You are a *liar!*"

Albert shook his head, sobbing. The boot came up from the right, and instinctively he warded it off with his right arm, though it knocked him sideways.

"Get up!" shouted the officer in a fury.

He was without hope.

"Get *up*, I said," the officer repeated.

He pushed himself up on his left arm. The door miraculously opened… oh God, was he saved?

"What is it?" asked the officer, impatiently.

It was the hawk-faced secretary. "There was just this," she said, holding the brooch. that Albert had given Lisel. "Near the bottom of the bag."

"Very well."

"Also, I apologize, Major, but we have a problem. There is a newsman who is screaming like a pig. We have spelled his name wrong. His arrest, he is saying, is a tragic mistake."

"That is ridiculous."

"I am sorry, Major, but Colonel Kostler has said to check. It seems there *have* been some errors."

Suddenly there was a great commotion in the hall. Through the half-open door, Albert could see a dark-haired man struggling with a guard. "Stay here," said the black-eyed officer to the secretary.

"But I am needed—"

"Oh this is bloody impossible!" To the black-eyed officer, Colonel Kostler's celebrated caution had been an endless source of aggravation, and the brownshirt round-up had brought out the worst of it. He turned to the young guard, whom he little respected. "Watch these," he said. "Carefully. This one, note, is *not* tied."

"Yes, sir."

The officer and the secretary left. The continued sounds of protest and resistance echoed down the hallway, then ended abruptly with the thump of a door.

The priest's eyes opened, and he gagged. The guard ordered silence, but the priest whispered, "Albert—"

"Shut your mouth, I say!" the guard shouted. His ferocity was real enough, but beneath it there was a weakness of inexperience and uncertainty.

"I am sorry," the priest whispered.

"Please," said the new suspect.

"Enough!" the youth ordered.

A look of terror gleamed in the suspect's eyes, below the new red bruises.

"He is my friend," he said in his high voice to the guard.

"I said *enough*," the uniform growled.

Looking at Albert, Konrad snapped his head back at the guard, who, hearing a shout outside, instinctively had turned in its direction. Understanding Konrad's advice, Albert, whose choices had been reduced to this, drove his shoulder into the priest's chair, wrapping his arms around its frame. The attack was as much a surprise to the battered and frightened suspect as it was to the young man.

"What are you *doing*?" the guard shouted in amazement, while the chair came at him and he was knocked, astonished, against the hard wall. His head slammed back and then forward. Albert fell head-long over the priest's shoulder, like a rescued man carried by a firefighter.

He scrambled in a nearly comic frenzy for the dropped revolver. He spun with it in one sudden motion, and drove it butt-first against the head of the stunned guard.

"Bastard!" Albert cried, as the boy slipped to the ground under the torrent of blows. "*Bastard*!"

He pounded till he couldn't, till he was exhausted and limp. Then, still in the hypnotic trance of survival, he wedged the back of a chair against the green door, under the knob. He surveyed the room like radar.

Weiss moaned to him. "Please."

But Albert heard nothing; he scooped up his possessions from the desk. Looked around again, his mind clicking through alternatives: ambush, direct flight…

Sounds outside.

He focused on the grey door by which the guard had stood.

Weiss pleaded. "At least kill us."

Konrad stared straight ahead, unmoving; the young guard had fired a muffled round into his back.

Again Weiss called, but Albert was at the door, then through it and pulling it closed behind him.

The black air where he found himself was vaguely putrid. He dug his lighter from his pocket and lit the space with a yellow flame. It was apparently a vestibule, windowless. There was another door ahead. He felt for the knob with his right arm, found it. He twisted at it clumsily, lighter still in hand but extinguished. The door was locked.

He relit the flame and knelt down with it at the large keyhole. He lay the lighter on the ground, still lit, and found the brooch in his pocket, opened it, slipped the pin into the keyhole, twisted it in the semi-dark without the slightest expectation of success. Outside in the hall he heard another argument. There were protestations and cries of a woman. "No!" he heard her at a distance. Something fell against the wall, just centimeters away from him but in another dimension.

In the dark lock, the pin compressed the back spring, and suddenly the door swung forward. He lost his balance and fell onto a stone floor. The brooch still in his hand, he closed it, put it in his pocket. He felt to his rear for the lighter, swept his left palm over the cool floor. As he found it, something rough squealed over his fingers.

He rose. There was a rectangle of grey light several meters up and away, and the putridity, which was now overwhelming, pushed down his throat and coiled in his stomach. He moved forward through the infested air toward the light, a window. He found his handkerchief and held it over his mouth and nose. Again a squeal, and something darted through his legs.

The grimy window was above his reach, but there were two or three shadowy crates under it, against the wall, and he stepped on a protruding crate-edge like a stair. The surface gave under his weight, and his left hand smashed into the topmost crate. He grabbed into it for support and pulled himself upright, but in his left hand was a strip of soft tissue, wet and rank. He looked under the loosened lid and saw in the shadows a ravaged face and torn shirt.

He gagged at the rotting corpse and the rank vapors. He stepped down and away, found his lighter and lit it. There were coffins, three of them, against the wall, and to the side, another corpse, of a young man. Two large rats were at his legs; they blinked at the yellow flame. The rest of the room was empty.

He was in a trance, moving trance-like through his motions. The husband, the father, the friend, the artist, even the Jew of him—he was none of these. Only a disengaged desire to escape. A rat had bounded to the top coffin, and he smashed it with his hand. The window his only hope; he climbed the little ziggurat of coffins. His bent knee pressed on the dead man's hideous belly. He cleaned the greasy window with his hand and his own saliva. He saw little, for the glass was as dirty on the outside as it was in. And the frame had been nailed into place.

He leaned his right shoulder against the wall and smashed at the window with the heel of his hand. He was beyond surprise, and he showed none when it broke. He pushed his right arm through the opening, folded his forearm around the outer sill. He found a corner in the frame for his left hand to grip and pulled himself upward and forward. In an incredible minute, he was out, in the sun, on a quiet Berlin side street.

He cleaned his face with his handkerchief; the bleeding had stopped. He dusted his sleeves and trousers. He wiped his cordovan shoes with his handkerchief. To his right, seventy-five meters away, two men in brown uniforms were prodded by black-clad SS. They looked in his direction, but he crossed and turned in the opposite way. His left hand began to ache from the blow the the window. Within a block, he hailed a taxi and drove to the Anhalter Station.

Back inside the greystone SS headquarters at 8 Prinz Albrechtstrasse,

Colonel Kostler detained the black-eyed officer for half an hour, and the Stormtrooper round-up, which produced a welter of confusion, provided the escaping Jew with the perfect diversion.

On the train, Albert traded for a change of clothes, including a black felt hat; and with an artist's touch, redid his bruised face. With luck and desperation, he slipped like a grain of sand through the hands of the SS. (The world in a grain of sand!)

When he awoke at nine that night, he had entered the Netherlands at the textile city of Enschede.

CHAPTER SIXTEEN

AFTER a drive to Bonn, Hitler had flown to Munich late on Friday the 29th, and he arrived at nearly four a.m. on Saturday, twelve hours before the anticipated "coup." He let Ernst Röhm stay sleeping in the Pension Hanselbauer at Bad Wiesse, a Bavarian gingerbread house on the Tehernsee Lake. Indeed, many in the Stormtroop ranks also slept in the small hotel. They slept in the arms of younger, lower-ranking Stormtroopers, or with the boys Granniger, the Nazi pimp, had sent them. They slept like the soldiers on leave that they were, exhausted by the debaucheries of peace.

Hitler let Röhm sleep until 6:30 that Saturday morning, when he banged on the hotel bedroom door. Rubbing sleep out of his eyes, Röhm opened the door to hear Hitler, furious in belted trenchcoat, screaming, "You're under arrest!"

It took a moment for Röhm to focus on the men with raised pistols standing behind Hitler. Pressing his chin into his neck to stifle a yawn, Röhm breathed out a welcoming salute. But the guns behind Hitler took hold of him and locked him up in the hotel basement along with other awakening Stormtroopers.

All over Germany that Saturday, the death lists were given to Hitler's SS assassins. The efficiency with which names on these lists were found was usually Sodom-like, although some generals, journalists, and wives were inadvertently mistaken for misspelled others and killed anyway. They were found, imprisoned, and shot. Or they were shot in their homes (hence the incidence of dead wives).

Back in Berlin, a housewife in the Lichterfelde suburb couldn't stand the rounds of incessant gunfire and screams from the nearby Cadet School where one hundred and fifty Stormtroop leaders were executed. She herself screamed until her husband drove her away to her family in Basdorf.

*

Lisel awakened the next day, Sunday morning of July 1st, in an old pension to which Horst had sent her. The house on the outskirts of Berlin tried to whisper its long history to her, but she had shut out the scenes and the voices by looking at the small bouquet of violets—oddly like the wallpaper bouquets at Albert's—that had arrived for her late on Saturday. She turned over in bed, smoothing her hair off her damp forehead. Albert must have arrived in Amsterdam by now, she prayed.

The bedroom was small and close although the window behind the lace curtains was open to the street. Two stories below, the slow sweeping morning sound rose of cows being led from the dairy next door. The cows lowed peacefully with relief, and the bells hanging under their thick loose necks tunked a dull rhythm. She had shut her eyes and sunk into the timeless peace of Sunday morning, of summer heat rising, of the cowbells and the cobbled streets. Then a car honked, stopped with the screeched irritation of brakes, and a heavy metal door opened and slammed shut. She knew that in several hours a car was to come for her. Indeed, she knew there was no escape from the century and the moment to which she had awakened.

At 2:30, she arrived at the festive tea party at the Chancellery in central Berlin. She wore the handful of violets pinned to the deep white collar of a black-and-white checkered dress. She moved about the garden in the mid-afternoon sun without her hat, whose close crown had made her feel too hot although its wide brim had kept the strong sun out of her eyes. She had laid the hat down on the wrought iron bench nearby. Now the sun had moved so the shadows were deeper under the broadleafed trees. Still, the sun's summer light seemed to make all the colorful flowers and green leaves glow. She was unaware that the light on her hair made her glow as well. Several people remarked upon her special radiance to Horst, who basked doubly in the sun and with pride.

There was about the afternoon the feeling of a festival altogether, following as it did the arrest and elimination of so many Stormtroop leaders. The Führer was in particularly high spirits, dividing his time between the small, arranged crowds in front of the Chancellery Building and his guests in the garden. He smiled benevolently at Goebbels's blond children playing tag through the Chancellery and onto the terrace. The boys wore white shirts and black shorts, and the girls were all in white dresses. The children played in the

Sunday summer heat without admonition, ignoring encouragements to eat some of the party sandwiches. Despite the heat, Hitler was neatly dressed in shiny black shoes, black slacks, white shirt, and black tie with his tan officer jacket decorated with the Iron Cross and a red swastika on the jacket sleeve. He stood on the terrace, drinking tea, surveying his guests and domain. Near him, within hearing, several people listened as one read aloud from an afternoon newspaper. In the article, a spokeman for the Army had given the Army's approval for the elimination of the many Stormtroop leaders:

> *On this momentous last Saturday in June, the Führer with soldierly decision and exemplary courage has himself attacked and crushed the traitors and murderers. The Army, as the bearer of arms of the entire people, far removed from the conflicts of domestic politics, will show its gratitude through devotion and loyalty. The good relationship toward the new Stormtroops demanded by the Führer will be gladly fostered by the Army in the consciousness that the ideal of both are held in common. The state of emergency has come to an end everywhere.*

Oberleutnant Wilhelm Brückner, Hitler's bodyguard, orderly, and aide de camp, looked over the reader and his audience and almost smiled. He turned and looked out at his master's garden. Despite the exhaustions of staying awake with the Führer since Friday, a rush of heat and pride filled Brückner. Nevertheless, he stood impassive like a high cement wall behind the much smaller man, Hitler. Brückner's weary eyes again scanned and surveyed the guests as the spasm of joy subsided into vigilence. He saw standing by a black iron bench under the trees a slender blonde woman and one of Dietrich's marksmen—Dörner was his name. Young Dörner's arm was loosely resting about the girl's waist in relaxed attention that Brückner approved with a pang, for the moment *was* triumphant. Now nothing stood in the Führer's way, he knew, now that the order for Ernst Röhm's execution had been phoned to Munich.

(In Stadelheim in prison in Munich, Röhm sat alone in his small cell, with a cot, a table, and a chair, and a small window that looked out upon his suddenly very small world.)

The beauty beside Dörner was smiling at the hard young officer and appeared to be teasing him about his gun, holstered tightly at his waist. Brückner heard her charming bird-like laughter, then rotated his attention elsewhere.

Lisel could feel the heat focused and mounting in Horst's revolver. She could feel the jarring pulses of the many times it had been fired in the previous day's Stormtrooper slaughter. She could feel the handling and balancing of reloading as her fingertips touched the shiny black leather that clasped the pistol. She could see and she could smell blood.

"Stop that, Sweetness," Horst said, patting her hand away. He shook his head also at her and held tightly onto her hand, whispering suggestively in her ear, "It's too soon so big a gun for so little a part of you."

She reddened and laughed and leaned her head against his hard uniformed shoulder. She coyly hid her face from

Horst until she felt him stiffen and followed his line of sight as Hitler descended the terrace to begin making rounds of the garden. She could feel all around her the spokes tighten around their center; let the Führer move and all about him iron filings magnetized to his will shifted and re-established palpable lines of force. Lisel swayed; Horst's palm pressed the small of her back. She closed her eyes. To be free of this earthbound binding, how she wanted to rise up on an air current with the birds in the garden! Then, with that thought, she felt herself flutter upward on a current away from Horst; she rose smoothly into the blue air.

(By three p.m. that afternoon of July 1, Ernst Röhm was dead, a suicide, his last words humming in the hot dense atmosphere, "*Mein Führer, mein Führer…*".)

In dark gusts of air that carried her backward, Lisel saw the image of Röhm, a shirtless fat man dead on stone. She felt then it was time.

(*Colibri*, the code word which had been used to set in motion the Stormtrooper purge, refers to Violetear hummingbirds: innately loyal creatures who form lasting bonds with their mates.)

Hitler waved the bird above his head away. Brückner glared at it. It caught the Führer's eye, hovering by a nearby pine branch. It trembled with new growth of light blue needles and silenced its cries that seemed to have carried it away from Hitler's fierce gesture. Only for part of a second more did the Führer fix his attention on the nervous little bird. Hitler felt the tic threaten in his right eye and the tightening down his right arm into an unconscious fist. A memory—of the 16th Bavarians—1914—the Belgian chateau where they'd been stalled, then been flushed out of thorny hedges—British gunfire—their Halloween—he could have died *that* day!—but no—this devil would have his day! Hitler righted himself and sauntered in front of Brückner about the garden.

Lisel wavered again. Mistaking her faintness for affection this time, Horst squeezed her waist. Then he looked into her pale face.

"Are you all right?" he asked.

Lisel tossed her head to shake off the weakness. She felt the pull of gravity back on the ground inside the embrace of Horst's strong grip. She felt the leather of the revolver holster press up against her hip. Lisel saw Hitler approaching and closed her eyes so he couldn't see, for now she knew he had many arms and eyes.

Horst saw the Führer approaching as well. He nodded down at Lisel.

"I understand, love," Horst said. "He weakens the knees of strong men. There is no shame in it." He moved his hand to caress her lovely hair and then cradled the back of her head in his palm.

She blessed the opportunity that Horst had given her; she leaned against him heavily, murmuring about the heat as well. The world which pressed against her was black and green, strong with the smell of sweating flesh and new-cut grass. Her hand moved down Horst's back as if groping for a handhold on a mountain from which she was falling—she could feel his tense embarrassment at her apparent collapse. But she had his gun.

Lisel slid to the grass at his feet, and in the black and white checkered folds of her skirt released the gun's safety with the practiced ease of another hand. Horst helped her to her feet; Hitler, with several others, moved forward with chivalric concern.

"Forgive me," she whispered. She looked into Hitler's dark eyes and with her left hand crossed herself. In an instant his black eyes recognized her, but it was too late.

The blue explosion—it must have come before the screams. In such moments even Time forgets itself and disorders events.

Hitler was thrown backward against his failed bodyguard.

Horst spun Lisel around, tore the hot revolver from her grip and screamed a word she failed to understand.

Brückner caught the blasted man. The tan military jacket, the Iron Cross, the white shirt and black tie—now a cordite-blackened, blood-soaked crater rim surrounded the pitted chest. At such close range, the gunshot had exploded the heart from the thorax. The giant Brückner, as if to cover the hideous pit, folded his hands, one over the other, above the charred and oozing cavity. In the green grass, red with blood, he ministered to the corpse.

Around the garden all motion had ceased except for the wind. All were silent except for the wildly singing birds. The men in uniforms were stunned into rigidity; all guns in the garden pointed at Lisel.

Time allowed a breeze to blow in the Chancellery garden. Then—Horst pulled the trigger of his recaptured revolver. Lisel collapsed in a heap of checkered cloth and crushed violets beside the black legs of the corpse that Brückner keened over.

"Arrest!" voices screamed, finally breathing in the moving air. "Arrest him! Kill him! Kill the traitor!"

"No no no," Horst moaned, the gun in his hand waving aimlessly in a pendulum sway back and forth above the garden grass. The young man tried to see what lay before him: the two objects of his passionate devotion, now red-soaked meat. Starlings twittered overhead. Their swooping flight suddenly reminded him of wider wings with greater shadows.

"No no no," he kept moaning. The closing, menacing circle of his fellows tightened around him and the pendulum sway of his rigid, armed hand rose up fast, as if the intended salute would prove his innocence—in another blur of blue and black and white smoke and sudden gust of red blood it was impossible again to tell if he had shot himself first or was shot by all the others.

It was only after the wind had cleared away the smoke that one could see, of the three bodies, the victim of misguided vengeance, was, as always, the most riddled.

That night, just after sunset, a crescent moon rose in Leo, like a smile.

CHAPTER SEVENTEEN

IN 1964, Dr. Anne Frank Koestler writes:

> *The journalist concerns himself with facts. The seeking-out and careful recreation of each fact is of vital concern to him. But the arrangement of the facts into a more than two-dimensional reproduction is not his concern. This is because he is a maker of accurate two-dimensional reproductions, and in this respect... journalism is his craft.*
>
> *On the other hand, the arrangement of brushstrokes into patterns that express... and communicate special meaning, this is art. And it is art that is the business, not of the journalist, but of the historian. For the historian (the true historian) is an artist; his brushstrokes, made from the pigments of life, create specially meaningful pictures of human affairs. What is most remarkable is that few, if any, truly understand that history is art, that the underlying craft of the historian to be in his own way. "Accurate" has nothing to do with the particular meaning he attempts not to find, but to create. Finally, of course, the corollary insinuates itself into our minds. If history is art, then in what way is art a kind of history? And further, in what sense might it also be, so-to-speak, "truer"?*

Thirty years earlier, in 1934, the newspaper accounts of Nazi murder and mayhem in Munich and Berlin were exactly what Frank Koestler has called "accurate reproductions." The American daily, *The New York Times*—which Albert's brother read in New York on the morning of July 1st—was journalism at is craftsman-like best. The meaning of the events, the symbolism and themes for the world, none of these were developed. The headlines and the story reported only the two-dimensional essence. Photos of Hitler, Röhm, and Lisel Ganz appeared from left to right.

HITLER KILLED A DAY AFTER CRUSHING NAZI RADICAL REVOLT: RÖHM A SUICIDE: VON PAPEN, VON BLOMBERG RESTORE ORDER

SHOT TO DEATH BY SOLDIER'S GIRLFRIEND

Triumph Turns to Disaster in Chancellery Garden
STORM TROOPS CHIEF DIES

HINDENBURG APPROVES VON PAPEN
Wireless to The New York Times.

BERLIN. July 1.—Only a day after the violent purging of rebels in the Stormtroops and reactionaries throughout Germany, Chancellor Adolf Hilter was shot to death by a young German woman, identified as artists' model Lisel Ganz, girlfriend of a young SS officer. The loss of the Nazi's supreme commander coupled with the purge of Storm Troop leadership must profoundly affect Germany's future. The purge of the Storm Troops, climaxed by the suicide today of their leader, Ernst Röhm, had been an action ordered yesterday by Chancellor Hitler to head off revolution, coup d'etat, or counter-revolution in Germany... Government leadership has passed to Vice-Chancellor Colonel Franz von Papen... President Hindenburg... has reported his approval.

The Official Version

The assasination today of Chancellor Hitler was preceded only by hours by the executions, suicides, and shootings that were explained in an official version Saturday as reaction to "a foreign power" threatening Germany with new national bolshevism.

The Beautiful Assassin

The motives of the artists' model Lisel Ganz remain a mystery. Whether she was acting alone or as an accomplice... raises questions about internal warfare, espionage, and revenge within Nazi ranks. A housecleaning of the Nazi inner-circle by the German Army is expected. Any connections Lisel Ganz may have had with communist or Catholic groups will also undergo investigation.

Stable Leadership Assured

Vice-Chancellor von Papen in Berlin... issued immediate assurances today...

CHAPTER EIGHTEEN

IN New York City, flocks of pigeons met for their own mass in front of the steps of Saint Patrick's Cathedral on the city's most fashionable thoroughfare. These were blue-and-grey birds whose necks in the bright sunlight had a pink iridescence it would have been difficult to render in paint on canvas. The occasional white pigeon was mottled blue, uglier than its fellows, but it would be easier under brush. The last Jew to flee the Nazi terror scattered the pigeons as he walked through their numbers to cross the busy avenue.

Albert Entrater had just left the dark, high-ceilinged cathedral where he had sat since the early morning, watching Christ hang from His golden cross. Having crossed Fifth Avenue, he looked up to observe the statue of Atlas bent to his knee under the dull brass rings of the world he struggled to uphold. A whisper in his mind recited from *Faust,* which he had obsessively read and re-read over the past four weeks: "By magic might before us doth appear/ massive enough, an ancient temple here/ Like Atlas who upheld the sky of old." So Faust watched over the artist of the New World. The chauffeured car that his brother had given him also waited protectively at the curb. He knew that if some policeman ordered the driver to move, the car would regain its expected place in orbit within a reliable time.

Albert walked farther into the square of brand new skyscrapers. Building was still in process on the most distant towers. The smell of new cement and the gnashing sounds of establishment-in-progress surrounded him. His brother Artur had an expression—"The city is growing up overnight"—that tightened Albert's chest muscles. Nevertheless, he was drawn to this, Rockefeller Center.

He stood above the lower court, his hand on the brass railing which gently burned against his palm in the August sun. The heat that had been unique as far north as Berlin was normal here in New York.

It had been two days since the popular German President Hindenburg died. Two days before that, there had been steady rain in New York. A relief rain of August. The weather had allowed him to sit alone nursing a sore throat in his brother's Long Island house. Since his arrival in New York, the days had blown by him like gusts building to a summer storm. But the days were not interested in him. They were busy with imperatives of their own convections, and no storm had broken. Just the steady two-day rain.

In his brother's house there was a large cooling unit throbbing in the dining room below and similar units throughout the house, but Albert kept the small windows in his room open. Alternately, he lay on the bed and stared at the ceiling, or sitting at a desk by the window, he drifted into a formless reverie. Always between him and a desired consummation came the figures of his lost friends.

Since Albert's arrival, his brother had treated him like someone newly released from a sanitarium. At the dinner table, he was seated beside his eight-year-old nephew. Artur's wife was clearly nervous about the visitor. Artur's mother, Albert's stepmother, was a stout woman who wore only flower-splashed black silk dresses. She was as wary of him now as she had been in his younger days.

From time to time, he could hear the sounds of his nephew playing baseball in the yard below. The boy spoke English with no accent, which pleased Artur. His nephew also spoke fluent German in the same accentless, high-pitched voice. But the only thing the child cared about was American baseball and a hero named Carl Hubbel, who had "struck out five in a row" in a so-called "All-Star Game."

When the boy had spoken of the stars, he distractedly began to recall Konrad's story of the Serpent Bearer, his favorite summer constellation. As his nephew pressed his ear to the large radio console, listening to the excited voice of a sports reporter, Albert had tried to recount the details of the wonderful myth. But then he suddenly heard himself yelling at the boy in furious German, and the boy's French *nourrice* interceded on the child's behalf. He realized he had not even known the nanny was in the room with them. It would be better to remove himself than to disturb the household, and Artur put at his service the chauffeur and car. Every day he was taken for a tour of the city on the pretext that he was seeking out a pleasant neighborhood to find a place to live, to have a studio. "You know perfectly well he could return to Berlin," he had overheard his step-mother say, "now that the Nazis are finished." Instead, he had for three weeks become a wanderer in a city in which rain seemed to cause the mushroom-eruption of towering buildings. *Planet* meant *wanderer*, Konrad had taught him.

Albert now stood above the courtyard in the new Rockefeller Center, facing a marble wall centered by a golden, eighteen-foot sculpture of Prometheus, apparently alighting on a ringed rock. Prometheus was in the center, flanked on either side by a bronze youth and maiden, the two who would receive the fire Prometheus upheld in his shining right hand. And where in this city, Albert wondered, was the other rock, the one Prometheus would be chained to? He idly touched the edge of a newspaper Artur had put in his hand the day his boat had docked. From that day, he had carried it with him everywhere. Artur had said, "I kept this for you," and what Albert might have seen first of his new country was lost in the reading of the July 1st news as reported to the New World.

Again, as he recalled the moment, he took the paper from his pocket to examine it once more. The pages were ragged at the edges, the print was smudged, but as ever, there were the three photographs: Röhm, Hilter… and Lisel. Her picture was a school photo. In it she looked like the young model who had appeared at his door only sixteen weeks earlier, not the woman he had left behind on the last day of June. It was the only likeness he had of her, save for the portrait in his mind. He carefully folded the paper into eighths and slipped it back into his pocket. He heard the nearby fountain gush and splash; the blinding gleam was gone from Prometheus.

He looked upward along the dizzying lines of the

surrounding towers. What he saw looked like a modern painting of converging parallel lines. The image told two stories in a wordless instant: first, he was a bird, trapped among the branches of overwhelming trees; second, he was Joseph, looking up from the bottom of the well.

Blinking and shaking his head, he then saw simply that the sky high above was clouding over. He looked to the left and right of the giant statue of Prometheus and saw the figures he had named Konrad and Lisel. Drops of rain began to fall with comic slowness. The August air was too heavy to move out of its way. A tourist in a straw hat turned his mouth upward to the sky to catch a drop of rain like a peanut. The comedy was a surprise to Albert. Like a long-lost voice, it touched him like the rain. The mood went further. His face looked conspiratorial as he decided he must escape. The black-uniformed chauffeur would be waiting to protect him from the coming weather. He began to walk east towards the underground railway, and he considered his condition.

What had he been doing these last several weeks? Even the limousine he sat in was cushion-covered. He was like some plump walnut secure inside a shell. With brief interruptions, that was an accurate appraisal of his whole life. Did his feet even touch the glitter-strewn cement of the sidewalks beginning to steam with rain? He did not feel them touch. Momentarily, he even felt invisible as he crossed Fifth Avenue. He was well out of the hindsight of his patient guardian. He came into view again at the next curb, where the buildings and shops reminded him of

Berlin. But no, the set was all too self-conscious and new to be anything but a copy for a European melodrama.

Invisible again for a block. No one could see the middle-aged man running, blown along in the increasing rain. He had to stop at a light at the avenue. He didn't see the wide grass islands; he saw instead Scotland heather. The tints of purple, pink, and blue moved in waves instead of the city street. When he moved, he moved because of the others. He was blown with the mass of heather-pollen and humanity. *"For He maketh His sun to rise on the evil and the good, and sendeth rain on the just and the unjust,"* he remembered Konrad's words.

He could see a block ahead in the downpour. It was an entrance to the safety of the underground. The wrought-iron sign overhead said *Lexington Avenue*. Rain washed over his face and down his cheeks. He ran down the dark cool steps and dug a nickel from his pocket for the wooden turnstile. The noise was hellish—it physically pushed at his body, but a wonderful eerie darkness surrounded him. A train for escape screeched to a metal stop. He took a seat on it. His fingertips touched the shiny, straw-woven seat.

As the doors were closing, Konrad slipped over the threshhold.

"Albert!" Konrad called. He swung his hand around a support pole and sat in the seat adjacent to him. He was out of breath. "Calm yourself, old friend. There now." He smiled. "After all."

"What did they do to you?"

"Less than you'd imagine."

The train gasped and sighed. It stopped. People stepped off and on. There was a shifting within an equilibrium that the acceleration of the train transformed into direction.

"God is richer than even you. Rest assured," Konrad said.

"I am not so certain there is a God."

"Better still. Then the goodness comes from us."

An elderly woman who sat across the aisle looked startled. She hugged her blue string bag lumpy with parcels and picked herself up heavily, swaying with the motion of the train to a more distant seat.

"There can be purpose where there is apparently no purposeful act."

"How?" Albert asked.

"If we make it so. That is the secret to see."

He hung his head onto his hand, balanced on his stumped arm. Both elbows were propped on his knees. Nausea and the train's lurching made him tremble.

"Perhaps I do *not* see."

Konrad answered with a sudden, sunlit smile.

Albert cupped his eyes which pooled with tears. He nearly fell forward as the train lurched to a stop. He looked out of reddened eyes at the now empty seat. He regained himself enough to sit back and find a handkerchief in the inside pocket of his jacket. He wiped his forehead, eyes, then mouth. A man who had taken a seat across the aisle leaned toward him.

"You okay, mister?"

He heard the English, understood.

"It's hard times," the man said.

"Yes… I am all right. Okay."

He found that day's newspaper, which a traveler had left behind. Hindenburg was still unburied. There was a reprint of the German President's will. Oddly, it was in German. Albert nodded when he read the passages that would contribute to a new Germany:

We deem it advisable that when we no longer serve, Chancellor von Papen reestablish a constitutional State, expressive and representative of the will of the German people...

...Again we repudiate the siege of barbarism and totalitarian state of the recent past; to this end, a separation of powers is advisable. The offices of the President and Chancellor are best divided and guided by the restoration of the monarchy we were so greatly honored once and for so long to serve.

The will ended with Hindenburg's personal farewell:

For our personal effects our truest wish is to be buried according to Christian service in Neudeck cemetery without laudatory speeches in a grave covered by a plain block of stone on which nothing but our name be inscribed. Let it be a cornerstone upon which the Royal State may ever rise.

Paul von Hindenburg
July, 1934

According to Chancellor von Papen (to think of von Papen as Chancellor!), this document was revised immediately after the "Night of the Long Knives" and the assassination of Chancellor Hitler on July 1st.

He looked over into the empty space. The helpful man across the aisle saw him turn pale, and he quickly took the seat at which Albert stared miserably.

"You got somewhere to go, buddy?" the man asked.

He looked blankly at the samaritan.

"You speak the language?" the man then asked in bad high-school German.

The traveler nodded.

"I think you lost being," the man struggled. "We just pulled Wall Street and these train doesn't stop up Clark in Brooklyn Heights, is perhaps at you are wenting?"

"I am not lost," he said slowly in perfect English, but he felt the words in his mouth like unchewed food.

"Where d'ya live?" the man asked.

Albert put his thumb in his mouth and began biting it.

"The thing to do is change at Clark Street back for the City and just stay on till 86th Street. That's where your people are," the man said, taking a scrap of paper from his pocket on which he wrote, over-large, the number 86. Albert nodded understanding and took out one of the business cards Artur had given him. On the back of the card he wrote the number 86 and gave it to the man. The old woman with the string bag of parcels stood close by, holding onto the pole by the door, evidently waiting for the next stop. She eavesdropped openly on the semi-conversation between the traveler and his guide, and once convinced of his German origin, she spoke in a rapid, triumphant Yiddish.

"Ha! The Devil is dead! *Yes!*"

With arch politeness Albert replied, "If *the* Devil is dead, madam, then God is dead and with Him all the angels."

The old woman and the man exchanged looks. She rubbed her temple in the universal sign for crazy, and the man nodded in agreement. Albert turned away from both, concentrating on the white tiles flashing past the subway window. The train ached and screamed into a station. The man touched Albert's knee and said in German, "Clark Street. You *out* get … and it *change*."

He stood, thanked the man, and followed the old woman out of the train with several others. She looked at him over her shoulder and in a surprising burst of energy disappeared up a flight of stairs away from the crazy man. Lost, he turned and looked back longingly at the train that contained one person who had offered help, only to see the man through the window pointing and nodding encouragement. Lightbulbs inside the train flickered and the doors closed.

He heard his heart in his ears now that the train had left. Then a pretty young woman with white-blonde braided hair was standing near him. He recognized her at once, and she smiled.

"I must go back. I was told."

She smiled again and nodded, then gave him directions and pointed. He bowed politely to thank her, still the twinkle of recognition in his eye. When he had crossed to the token booth, he turned to look at her again. Of course, she was watching him. Then, suddenly, she waved.

He followed the directions and walked upstairs to the platform facing where she had stood. She was gone. But he knew now he was supposed to go to 86th Street for some special reason.

The downpour had stopped by the time he walked up the steps and stood on the corner of 86th Street and Lexington Avenue. There were deep puddles at the curbs, and vapor rose like clouds from the cement sidewalks. He stood at the corner trying to reestablish the mental compass he had lost. He saw a flower-seller's shop. Next to the rain-soaked flowers was a newspaper stand. There he saw the German papers, and the voices of the words leaped into his mind. What a relief—he was back in Berlin again!

By the headlines, he could see which paper was Nazi: the *Deutscher Weckruf und Beobachter* called Hindenburg's will "Treason!". The anti-Nazi *Deutsches Volksecho* carried a photograph of Hindenburg lying in state and proclaimed "The People's Will!". *The Staats-Zeitung und Herold* reported "Funeral Tuesday." He sniffed the still-humid air from the Havel and Spree. He bought six newspapers at the stand and held them all under his arm, close by his body.

He heard the eager and anxious German voices as people raced about the noisy elevated train that was a pride of Berlin. The typical Berlin shops continued along both sides of the street. The buildings were three and four stories high, and nearly all had stores on the ground level. There was the familiar outdoor café where men sat drinking large steins of beer. He breathed in the steaming cabbage and wurst. A bakery window offered a shiny wheel of bread.

A market window offered soap and coffee. "This is what these people call a 'Depression' and they still call themselves German," he whispered.

A sweet arrow from childhood, the fragrance of marzipan, pierced him. He stopped, turned, and sighted the target, a narrow store whose shelved cases were filled with candies. As soon as he entered, it smelled like heaven. At the back of the store, in hearing and view was a table at which three men sat, apparently friends of the proprietor. As he examined the counter, the men kept on with their conversation which had been briefly interrupted when his entrance through the screen door had rung a shiny brass bell. Keeping one ear open to the talk and one eye on him, the owner busied himself rearranging the countertop where decorated tins of candies were stacked in little pyramids.

"Well, you say that because you got a job," one voice grumbled in the accent of a true Berliner.

"It's good to see you back here," said another.

The first voice fairly growled, "You see, it's women! I told you, I told you before it ever happened, the cook didn't like us, anti-Nazi she was, the little bitch from Freiburg—"

"From Freiburg she was?" the third one interrupted. "I have a cousin in Braunlingen."

"The cook didn't like us," the angry voice continued, "and another bitch kills the Führer, and if that is not enough to break the heart of a true man, the pin in my lapel," there was a pause during which he fingered his Nazi insignia, "they see the pin in my lapel which I am *not* about to remove and the Jew fires me, me and the wife, right in the middle of the day, half wages, go to hell!"

"The cook was Jewish?"

"Not the cook," the voice yelled. "The owner, you idiot!"

"You never liked the Westchester, anyway," the third voice soothed.

"You can talk easy, you got yourself a job," the man repeated more calmly. "The Führer would've taken care of them, I'll tell you. He had a plan. And now what've we got? Business as usual. Jew business as usual!"

"I don't have a job either," one said. "Deitrich does, but I don't."

"You're a Jew-lover, you'll do just fine," the Nazi muttered.

"I don't love, I don't hate," came the response.

"That's the best thing in the long run," the third said. "Live and let live."

"Oh!" the Nazi barked. "That's what's wrong with this goddamn country!" And he left the store by a back door everyone heard slam.

The proprietor offered his palms up to his customer by way of apology. Albert put the newspapers down on a place cleared on the counter, and began pointing at candies.

"A man out of work isn't always reasonable," the owner said. He tied up the box of candies and accepted payment, careful not to look at the handless arm.

"The Great War?" he said kindly.

Albert nodded.

"I lost two brothers."

He put the box of candies back down on the counter and reached into his pocket and drew out a business card. He gave it to the puzzled store owner.

"Tell them to call my brother," he said. "*Including* the Nazi."

The man looked at the card, then whistled through his teeth, a sound which mingled with the ringing of the shiny brass bell as Albert left. Now that he had the newspapers and the candy box to manage, he tucked the papers under his short arm and held the candy by its string in his fingers. He knew just what to do. It was clearer by the minute. On the other side of the street, the four-story brownstones continued. One had a tailor's shop. Above the store was a deep bay window. It was an ideal location for an artist's studio.

He stood on Prinzregentstrasse looking up at the windows of his studio. His throat burned; his face was hot. As he stared blindly at the building, he heard a boat's horn. It was bright and piercing, and it made him turn east toward the water. He realized how close he was to the Spree and then saw with delight the tips of the masts. They were moving south past the treetops of what was a waters-edge park. After a surprisingly short walk, he was at the entrance to the park, looking up at the circling birds. It was a tranquil Saturday in August after all. He found just the place beyond one of the low hills that greened along the banks. He sat. His legs were tired and aching. His heart throbbed. The grass was still damp from the rain. He could hear his father's voice scolding against sitting on wet ground or cold stone. *"Do not invite rheumatism!"* The old man had died without a creak or a cringe.

Obediently, he spread out all his newspapers like a blanket on the grass. Carefully, he opened his box of special candy. The air swept in from the water, which was the amber that appeared in so many of his paintings. He pressed his lips into the soft candy, and all the holidays of childhood tasted in his mouth. He breathed crushed almonds and Mother's perfume. He opened his eyes after this rapture and looked down the long green slope. From where he sat, he could see in the near distance of a mile or two another marina toward which a shining sailboat moved. The August wind warmly blew the boat on the glitter-finned fish that was the river, leaping over and under and south around its elemental self.

This—this was the moment he had sought. The perfect moment.

He contined to nibble on the white bottom of a marzipan pear. His concentration on the candy was not lost upon a little girl of perhaps three, who was walking along the path some meters from his legs. He heard her mother's shushings before the child actually materialized before him, kneeling on the edge of his newspaper picnic blanket, holding out her palm prettily, saying, "Thank you, please."

Lovely Hilde, in navy white-collared dress, quickly caught up with her and begged his pardon. He didn't stand. He realized he couldn't.

Instead, he reached into the box and handed them each one of his candies. He spoke to them in German. Then he started to laugh and the child giggled. All excited, she performed her repertoire of scary faces for him. When she was done, she popped a marzipan apple, whole, into her mouth. She noticed his missing hand. She quickly looked at the hand that held another piece of candy.

"Does it hurt?" Gerta asked.

"Only sometimes," he said.

"God bless you," she said, as if he had sneezed.

The child then followed her mother away. He felt greatly tired. He lay back on the newspaper and it seemed to whisper in his ears. On his back, he watched the last of the rainclouds blowing away in purple billows to the southeast. It was painful to look blankly at the bright afternoon sky. His eyes watered. He shut them and slept.

When he opened them again, the bowl of night was gathering above him, a thing of such beauty, he gasped.

"It's all right," a familiar voice said above him. "Thank God, I was called."

Jupiter would still be full tonight, bright and wise. Mars and Saturn would be diminished to their waning halves, close by Virgo. The waxing half-moon would beam by Saturn's left hand.

"Virgo stands like St. Michael at the end of the universe," he told people who were moving about him. A few fireflies were twinkling in the parks. The stars were all rising in the sky. He was standing up and being led somewhere. It was getting dark and street lamps illuminated a row of red townhouses with shiny black doors and brass doorknobs so dimly that the scene looked as two-dimensional as a painting.

"It's really hot as hell, isn't it?" he said.

Overhead, Vega thrummed in the Lyre and Deneb was the burning eye of the black, bejeweled Swan. There was a humming and burning inside him; he swayed against the body that supported him. Then he was leaning against a soft corner. What he saw in front of him was the frame of a car window around the finished canvas of *The Park at Night*, stars and moon rising overhead, the Spree in the distance in the wavy threads of low rotating clouds. In the foreground in the yellow lamplight, backgrounded by black and green-illuminated trees, were two shadowy figures.

It was Virgo and lost Pollux! They were clothed in white and glittering stars that made him blink. A dry cool hand pressed against his burning forehead. He drew a breath at the touch. He closed his eyes and sank into the coolness, and when he opened them again, he saw Lisel and Konrad standing on a rise under the lamplight under the trees. At the horizon he could see the last of the light shining through them.

Lisel raised her transparent arm—Konrad did the same. They were smiling at him and waving goodbye. He lifted his arm heavily. With his ghost hand he returned their farewell. Then he leaned against his brother and gave himself up to the unconsciousness shared by the millions of other survivors.

*

Three decades later, Columbia University history professor Anne Frank-Koestler met the artist through mutual expatriate friends at the gallery show where she admired his painting *The Park at Night* and wished aloud that she could afford it. Having equally enjoyed a book of Prof. Frank-Koestler's, Albert Entrater arranged to make the purchase possible. Thus began the dialogue between them that led to her research into this narrow corner of modern German history she called “a mercifully quieted cul de sac” and which resulted in her Pulitzer Prize-winning work, *The Right of Way*, which linked the highway of history with the avenue of art, and thereby inspired this novel.

CPSIA information can be obtained at www.ICGtesting.com
Printed in the USA
BVOW06s0030250716

456704BV00021B/149/P

9 789881 219695